TRAGEDY IN PARADISE

When Texas Ranger Captain Brad Saunders is sent to investigate a fence war in Lascelles County, he finds a distraught blind girl wandering alone. Appalled to discover that her family have been wiped out, Brad sets out to find the killers. He uncovers a web of murderous intrigue against the girl's father, who had led the fence-cutters. The conspiracy involved respectable Judge Banyon and an outlaw posing as a Texas Ranger. The blind girl was a witness, but would that be enough to prove that Brad himself was not the murderer?

Doncaster
Council

DONCASTER LIBRARY AND INFORMATION SERVICES
www.doncaster.gov.uk
Please return/renew this item by the
last date shown.
Thank you for using your library.

InPress 0231 MAY 18

D. A. HORNCASTLE

TRAGEDY IN PARADISE

Complete and Unabridged

LINFORD
Leicester

First published in Great Britain in 2001 by
Robert Hale Limited
London

First Linford Edition
published 2003
by arrangement with
Robert Hale Limited
London

British Library CIP Data

Horncastle, D. A.
    Tragedy in paradise.—Large print ed.—
Linford western library
    1. Western stories
    2. Large type books
    I. Title
    823.9'14 [F]

    ISBN 0–7089–9964–6

Published by
F. A. Thorpe (Publishing)
Anstey, Leicestershire
Set by Words & Graphics Ltd.
Anstey, Leicestershire
Printed and bound in Great Britain by
T. J. International Ltd., Padstow, Cornwall

This book is printed on acid-free paper

For Julie

For we walk by faith, not by sight.
Corinthians II 5:7

1

'The Governor will see you now, Lieutenant Saunders.'

Brad stubbed out his cigarette and sprang to his feet, eager for action after some twenty minutes spent sitting on a leather-bound chair in an anteroom.

The Texas State Governor's private secretary paused as he reached the doorway to the inner sanctum. He was tall and thin with the stoop and pallid complexion of a man who had spent his entire life indoors. He regarded Brad myopically over his wire-framed, half-moon spectacles with the air of a schoolmaster about to usher a recalcitrant pupil into the presence of his headmaster.

'Please to remember that the Governor is addressed as 'Your Excellency',' he said.

'I'll do that, Mr Peagood,' Brad

replied, trying hard to conceal his amusement.

The secretary opened the door and ushered Brad into the office. 'Your Excellency, this is Lieutenant Saunders.'

'Thank you, Peagood.' The reply came from behind the biggest desk Brad had ever seen in his life. 'You may leave us, please.'

Brad heard a click as the door was closed discreetly behind him. He had no time to appraise the man in front of him or the room he was sitting in, for Governor Oran P. Roberts finished scribbling his signature on a document, slid it to one side and then, grabbing a smouldering cigar from an ashtray, he regarded Brad with a penetrating stare.

'So, at long last I have the pleasure of meeting the man who exposed that horse-stealing racket at Silver Springs,' he said. 'That was a nasty business. Judge Dungannon speaks very highly of you, Lieutenant Saunders.'

Brad shifted uncomfortably. His right

hand strayed towards the pocket in his vest where he kept his Bull Durham sack but he hastily withdrew it.

'I'd offer you a cigar, lieutenant, but my bet is you're a Bull Durham man,' the Governor said with a smile. 'So go ahead.'

He paused while Brad fished out the makings and lit up.

'Well, now, I can see you aren't a man who takes to praise easily,' the Governor continued, 'and I respect you for that. So I'll get to the point of this meeting straight away. Tell me, how do you see your future, Lieutenant Saunders?'

The directness of the question caught Brad on the hop.

'Well, the frontier ain't the place it used to be, I guess,' he drawled.

'Do you believe things are getting better?'

Brad nodded. 'We're gettin' there, slowly but surely. And that's no bad thing, I guess. Why, I even get to figurin' I might resign from the Rangers one day and look for a proper job.'

'Can't say I blame you. Which is why I've ordered you to be relieved from your command forthwith.' The Governor smiled as Brad's jaw dropped open. 'Don't get me wrong, lieutenant, let me explain.'

Governor Roberts sat back in his chair and removed a fleck of tobacco from his lower lip.

'You boys have done an excellent job along the frontier,' he continued. 'But now that Major Jones has died, that role is now changing. The Indians have been defeated and Mexico has learned to live with the *status quo*. The heyday of Captain McNelly and his Special Force is over, but we aren't out of the wood yet. What I am seeking to do is widen the Rangers' remit to cover the whole of Texas. I want the service to provide back-up for the existing framework of law-enforcement wherever the need arises. We need men who are capable of acting alone, using their initiative at the highest level. I believe that you are one such man.'

'Have you any particular job in mind?' Brad enquired.

'You see these? They are letters of complaint about the excessive and unreasonable use of barb-wire fencing.'

Brad took a sharp intake of breath. He had been in San Antonio back in '76 when John 'Bet-a-Million' Gates had demonstrated the effectiveness of the new invention in the Military Plaza.

Jaunty, cocksure, Gates had asserted that his fence would be 'pig-tight, horse-high and bull-strong' and proceeded to demonstrate its effectiveness before a sceptical audience of ranchers and farmers. Cowmen were buying land from the state and enclosing it. That Texas was short of fencing materials was self-evident and barb-wire was the answer.

'It's causing problems everywhere,' the Governor continued. 'But things are getting out of hand in Lascelles County. There's complaints coming in that the

5

big ranchers are fencing off waterholes, even main access trails. Their opponents, mainly smaller fry, who can't afford to buy wire, are banding together to cut the fences. And now I understand the ranchers are contemplating taking the law into their own hands to protect their interests. There's talk of bringing in hired guns.'

'Can't the local law take care of it?' Brad enquired.

The Governor frowned. 'It appears not to be the case. Your average sheriff or town marshal can handle the small-time criminal element, but they seem at a loss as to how to handle powerful vested interests.'

'That don't surprise me,' Brad opined, 'considerin' such interests probably had a mighty big say in their appointment.'

The Governor shot Brad a keen glance as he rose and began to pace to and fro.

'As State Governor, I have to take account of the broad picture. I am laying plans to build the finest capitol building in the country and these people are making me look a laughing-stock. I can just guess what they're saying back in Washington: 'Oran Roberts believes he's taming the West and they're making a monkey out of him.' Well, I'm not running with that, Lieutenant Saunders, I can assure you.'

'I get your drift,' Brad said. 'But this sounds like a job for a company.'

The Governor shook his head. 'We aren't dealing with Indians and Mexican border thieves; we're dealing with our own people — Texans. One way or another, these people have to learn that the rule of law holds sway. I want you to go to Lascelles County alone, assess the situation and take whatever action you feel is necessary to resolve it. Is that understood?'

Brad nodded.

'There is one thing I should mention. In my role as State Governor, I don't have any executive responsibility. You must understand that you are acting

7

solely in your capacity as peace officer for the State of Texas. That is why this meeting has not been minuted by my secretary.'

When Brad nodded, Governor Roberts gave a grim smile. 'You're a man of few words, I guess, but I have every faith in you. In that respect I have to tell you that I believe you will find that you have been promoted to the rank of captain forthwith.'

Before Brad could reply, the Governor hit a bell on his desk.

'Captain Saunders is leaving now, Peagood,' he said as the door opened.

As Brad shook hands with the Governor and left the inner sanctum it amused him to see the shocked look on the secretary's face as he stubbed out his cigarette in the silver ashtray on the Governor's desk.

And, as it happened, he hadn't called the Governor anything . . .

★   ★   ★

The private gaming-room in the upper storey of the Cattleman's Club in Paradise, the county seat of Lascelles County, was at this moment in time being put to a somewhat different use. It was hosting a meeting of three determined men hell-bent on dividing the county's land between them.

'Well, gentlemen, I believe we are now in a position to take the initiative,' Judge Banyon said.

Thin as whipcord, a black eye-patch gave the owner of the Bar B Ranch a sinister aspect. The son of a New York police officer, he had trained as a lawyer. When war broke out he joined the Army of the Potomac, rising to the rank of major in an infantry regiment, and suffered an eye injury at Bull Run. Unable to face working in a lawyer's office, when the war ended, he had come out West to seek his fortune. Here, his energy and determination had seen him through to his present position as a mainstay of the local community.

Judge Banyon settled back in his leather armchair, drew heavily on his Havana cigar and exhaled, sending wreaths of smoke coiling upwards to shroud the gilded chandelier above him.

Nathan Cowper sipped his whiskey and regarded Banyon over the rim of his cut-glass tumbler through hooded eyes. He owned the Double C spread, inherited from his father. His military service during the war had been confined to organizing the commissariat in a Confederate base camp. The only shots he had heard fired were at a practice range. A big bald man, gone early to seed, his body moulded comfortably to the depths of an armchair. Heavy jowls gave him the appearance of a man appreciative of the pleasures of life.

However, in matters of business, Nathan Cowper was far from lethargic. As president of the Cattleman's Association and mayor of Paradise, it irked him to be indebted in any way to this cocksure bantam of a man who, by virtue of his military background, seemed to have assumed leadership as of right.

'So the Rangers have agreed to come?' he said heavily.

'There was never any doubt about it in my mind that they would refuse,' Banyon remarked.

'We canna be seen to be breaking the law,' the third man agreed. A Scotsman and a man of few words, David Fife was the manager of the Lazy Z, a spread owned by an Edinburgh-based invest-ment consortium.

Banyon paused until the sloe-eyed Hispanic waitress who set up the whiskey glasses on a silver salver had withdrawn from the room. He smiled inwardly at Nathan Cowper's lascivious glance. Banyon made it his business to find the fatal chink in a man's armour in order to bring about his downfall. Reading Cowper was easy — Fife was a problem because he was a lay preacher and a pillar of the community.

11

'So it's agreed we leave it to the Rangers, then?' Banyon allowed himself the luxury of a thin smile as he spoke.

Cowper flicked ash from his cigar as he nodded approval, but behind those hooded eyelids Banyon figured Nathan Cowper was not a happy man.

★　★　★

A purplish mist, veiling the land with ghostly images, ringed the hills surrounding Austin as Brad left the city early the following morning. The Chisholm Trail passed through the eastern part of the city. A convoy of three heavy wagons, each carrying bales of cotton, rumbled along Congress Avenue.

Brad was wearing range clothes. Sitting on board the hurricane deck of his magnificent stallion, Blaze, he had decided to travel under an assumed name, his badge of office pinned discreetly inside his vest.

He had not delayed his departure, for

he had a long journey ahead. Lascelles County was in the heart of the Texas Panhandle. Born on a ranch on the High Plains, Brad was used to wide open spaces and the limitless horizons of the northernmost part of the Lone Star State.

But then the war had come and service with Jeb Stuart, the legendary Confederate cavalry commander, had influenced his subsequent life. During that bloody conflict, he had moved seamlessly from boy to man without the breaking-in experience of adolescence.

When the war ended Brad, burned up with the bitter taste of defeat and after a spell of stock detecting, had joined the re-formed Texas Rangers. The free and easy ways of this paramilitary organization had proved his salvation. It gave him freedom of thought and action and a sense of responsibility. Gradually he had become integrated into a society he had come to despise and reject. In short, he had recovered his self-respect and had come to realize that without it, a man is worthless both to himself and everyone else.

That night he camped underneath a sky glistening with stars. By the light of a camp-fire, Brad wrote his sister, Beth, a short letter. He made no mention of his mission.

When he had finished it, he tucked it into an envelope and slipped it into his vest pocket.

As he leaned forward to stir the embers of the fire, the full meaning of his promotion struck him. He was no longer just a Texas Ranger; he was the State Governor's special representative in Lascelles County.

'I guess you've come a long way, Brad-boy,' he told himself.

★　★　★

One week later, Brad reined in his horse to read a sign which said:

WELCOME TO LASCELLES COUNTY
PARADISE 32 MILES.

14

The breeze scarcely relieved the shimmering heat haze hanging over the sea of grass spread out in front of him. The flatness was an illusion, for in reality the terrain was undulating, giving the impression of false horizons. The August sun stood half-mast glaring out of a sky of washed-out blue. From this point on the main trail was flanked on either side by a gleaming barb-wire fence. Exactly at the site of the sign, each fence broke away right and left, clearly delineating the county line.

For a man like Brad, born and raised on the open range, the spectacle did not appeal. The fences seemed an affront, an unwelcome reminder that the hand of man was everywhere. In a rare moment of vision he perceived there would come a day when there would be no wild places left.

Five miles down the trail he detected a movement in the sea of grass that waved in the warm breeze. Puzzled, he reined in. A man travelling on his own had best have all his wits about him.

He took out the brass-bound spyglass he always carried in a leather pouch on his gun belt and examined the landscape. At first, nothing stirred in the shimmering heat haze — but then, there it was again . . .

Holding Blaze rock-steady, he focused the eyepiece.

He removed it, shaking his head in disbelief, before trying again.

There was no doubt about it — there was someone out there beyond the fence — a young woman. She was on foot, with no sign of any transport.

Snapping the 'scope shut he replaced it. There was no sign of a horse. In the West, no one went about on foot. Without further ado, he set Blaze at the fence, approaching it at an angle on account of the narrowness of the trail, and cleared it easily.

As he suspected there was no recognizable trail leading to his quarry. The woman appeared to be wandering around aimlessly.

He took Blaze forward without

undue haste. As he drew closer, she detected his presence. For a moment she stood as if rooted to the spot, but then she uttered a terrified cry and broke into a run.

'Wait!' Brad called out.

He dismounted and ran after the woman with giant strides. Just as he caught up with her, she tripped and fell face down in the grass. As Brad reached out to help her to her feet, she cringed from him, her face distraught. Her clothes were intact and she showed no sign of ill treatment.

Brad sat down beside her, took out the makings and rolled a smoke. The naturalness of the act seemed to calm her. She sat on a tussock in a declivity in the ground and regarded Brad with a blank expression that made him feel uneasy to a degree he would never have thought possible. She was very young, little more than a girl, perhaps still in her early teens. That something bad had happened was self-evident. It was going to take a good deal of patience to find out what.

'Stay right where you are,' he said. 'I'll go get you some water.'

He kept her in view out the corner of his eye while he fetched his water-bottle.

When he came back, he unscrewed the cap and offered it to the girl. She hesitated.

'Take it,' he said, gently putting it into her hands. When she hesitated he said, 'It's only water.' She almost snatched it from him. Recollection from the past stirred in Brad's mind as he watched her. She was drinking in the same uncontrolled way men did after fighting in a battle. Terror aroused an almost unquenchable thirst. That much he had become acquainted with when he had been little more than a boy himself.

'I'm Frank Rio,' he said gently when the girl had finished. 'I'm a stranger to these parts. Like to tell me what's happened?'

She opened her mouth to speak, but the words wouldn't come. The only sound was the sough of the wind in the grass.

'Take your time,' Brad said. 'I ain't in no hurry.'

The girl tried again and failed. Although the sun was searing hot, she was shivering.

'Won't you tell me your name?' Brad asked. When this failed to produce a response he continued, 'How about I take you home? Show me the way. It can't be far.'

His suggestion produced a reaction he didn't anticipate. The girl sat huddled on the ground, tears streaming down her face.

'You had problems with your ma and pa?' Brad enquired. 'You won't be the first, you know,' he concluded lamely.

Hell's teeth, he thought, I ain't getting anywhere here. What am I gonna do?

He stood up and surveyed the landscape again. The trail to Paradise was way out of sight; there was no sign of human habitation. There was only one thing left for it: he would have to backtrack the girl's movements in order to find out where she had come from.

'We gotta move,' he said. 'You can't stay here.'

He moved over to Blaze. 'You can ride with me on the hoss if you like,' he offered.

The girl neither spoke nor moved. She sat on a rocky outcrop staring ahead.

In a quandary, Brad set forth on foot, leading Blaze after him, reading sign until he had a clear picture of the route the girl had followed. When he returned, she hadn't moved.

'Come on. We gotta go now,' Brad said gently.

He walked over to Blaze, took the reins and began to follow the girl's tracks back through the grass. For a few anxious moments he figured she would not move, but then, suddenly, he saw her get up and, after a moment's hesitation, to his relief, begin to follow him.

Like most men born and bred in the West, Brad was no walker and he plodded on for a mile or so until he came to a slight rise in the land. Ahead ran a narrow winding trail. As he waited to allow the girl to draw nearer he noticed a faint wisp of smoke on the horizon. He drew out his telescope and focused it. A clear image of a house jumped into view.

'That where you live?' Brad enquired. The lack of response was of no consequence to him for he knew the answer. The sign told him all he needed to know. He moved on. By the time he hit the trail he knew the girl had come from the direction of the house that lay about a mile away.

As he drew closer, the land dipped again to reveal a wide creek-bed sparkling with a thin runnel of water. Beyond it lay another wire fence separating it from some fields with growing crops.

He paused, puzzled. What the hell was going on? The house lay on the opposite side of the creek. To use the trail from the house, there must be a way through the fence.

There was no gate.

From the opposite side of the creek he saw that where the trail went through, there was no wire, because it had been cut. The loose strands had been pushed clear to allow free passage. He surveyed the scene grimly. Clearly someone had attempted to separate the house and its occupants from the creek — and to bar access to the main trail to Paradise.

Sign showed evidence of the recent passage of a small herd of maybe a couple of dozen cattle and horses through the creek on to the range beyond.

The girl was still behind him, hanging back. Brad crossed the creek on foot and waited for her to follow him.

There was something about the way

the girl moved which puzzled him . . . a hesitancy . . . and then suddenly he could have kicked himself for not realizing something he should have spotted right from the start.

She was blind.

When she was safely across the creek he moved with a greater certainty and continued on until he reached the house.

The house was a typical sodbuster's dwelling. Constructed with adobe walls and a sod roof from which clumps of wild flowers sprouted in incongruous profusion. Half a dozen chickens scratched about in the yard, unconcerned at his approach.

Despite the peaceful situation, Brad was suddenly overtaken with a sense of foreboding. He was convinced that something bad had happened here.

He walked slowly up the path to the house. The door, hanging on leather hinges, stood ajar. He pushed it open and looked inside. It was a typical one-room cabin. The floor was of packed earth.

All the signs revealed recent occupation. A cooking-pot had burned dry on the dying embers of the fire, revealing the charred remains of a beef stew. A clock ticked quietly on a shelf in the corner. A rumpled newspaper lay on the bottom of a crudely made wooden chair.

He came back outside and looked for the girl, but she was nowhere to be seen. Had she run away again? He cursed under his breath for his carelessness. As he turned the corner of the house he heard the sound of sobbing.

What Brad saw next brought him to an abrupt halt. He had seen many disturbing sights in his life but what he saw now made his blood run cold.

Three corpses swung gently in the breeze. They were suspended from a crudely fashioned cross-beam over the doorway of a barn. Their feet made a slight scraping noise as they brushed the ground. The unsynchronized movements gave them a macabre animation all their own.

'My father, my mother and my brother.'

The sound of the girl's voice speaking for the first time unnerved Brad. Instinctively, he slipped his arm protectively about her narrow shoulders.

'I will find who did this,' he vowed. 'And I will make them pay.'

2

Brad took the girl back into the house. Then he set about the task of making some coffee.

By the time it was ready she had stopped crying. She was sitting on a wooden chair, staring ahead with her sightless eyes.

The shock of what he had just seen was still with him but, sensing he was more in control of himself, Brad said, 'Will you tell me your name?'

'Lisa Warrender,' came the reply.

'I believe you are blind, Lisa,' he said gently.

She nodded. 'Since birth — I can only tell the difference between light and dark.'

'I know it's hard for you, Lisa, but before I bury your folks, will you tell me what happened?'

The girl took a deep breath and then

the words came tumbling out with a rush.

'It was all so quick. We'd just finished breakfast and I was feeding the chickens in the yard when I heard the sound of riders. I heard voices, my father's, my brother's — and my mother's, too. I hid in the barn. I could hear what was happening . . . '

'How many men were there?' Brad could have kicked himself for asking such a specific question.

The girl answered without hesitation. 'Three. They dragged my parents and my brother round to the barn. My father pleaded with them to spare my mother. They took it in turns to rape her. I could hear them. They were laughing as they did it. Then they hanged them before they rode off with our stock.'

Hardened as he was, Brad felt his blood run cold.

'How come they didn't see you?'

'I hid. When they had gone, I just wanted to get away.'

Brad's coffee, although initially welcome, suddenly lost its savour.

'How could you stay here after that?' he said. 'You were very brave to come back with me. Tell me, Lisa, have you any idea who did this and why?'

'Judge Banyon claims he owns all the land round here. He rode over here several weeks ago and ordered Pa off what he claimed was his land. When Pa refused, he fenced off the creek to stop us from getting water. Pa cut the wire. He had to. Without water our crops would fail and our cattle would die.'

'Do you know the names of any of the men who killed your folks?'

The girl shook her head. 'They were strangers.'

'How can you be sure?'

'Because I heard one man asking how far they were from Paradise.' She hesitated. 'My father wrote several letters to the Governor requesting that the Rangers be sent in to restore law and order. But he heard nothing and now I guess it's too late.'

Brad winced at the implied rebuke.

'What about the local law?' he enquired.

'Sheriff Rance? Pa said he was in the pockets of the big cattlemen.'

That figures, Brad thought.

'Do you have any relatives or friends who can look after you?'

'My grandparents live in Paradise. Grandpa owns the hardware store.'

Brad walked over to the door.

'You'll find a spade in the barn, Mr Rio,' the girl said. 'Meantime I will get some food ready.'

Brad found the girl's prescience unnerving. He soon found the implement and set about the melancholy task of cutting down and burying the corpses. He fashioned three wooden crosses from some timber and was hammering the last one into position when he became aware that she was standing beside him.

'Do you know any prayers, Mr Rio?' she said when he laid aside his spade.

'Only The Lord's Prayer, I guess,' he replied.

'Then please say it with me.'

When they finished, Brad accompanied the girl back into the house.

She ladled out a fresh beef-stew from the cooking-pot. Brad didn't feel hungry, but he forced himself to eat it, knowing he would need all his strength for what lay ahead.

'It's getting late, Mr Rio,' Lisa said. 'We must leave for Paradise tomorrow morning.'

Brad marvelled at her self-possession. She was right, of course.

'How old are you, Lisa?' he enquired.

'I'll be fifteen next week.'

Brad went outside to Blaze and retrieved his bedroll. When he returned to the house the girl was on her knees praying silently in front of a crucifix nailed to a wall.

* * *

Brad awoke the following morning to the sound of hammering. As he rose, he saw that Lisa was already up and dressed. The smell of coffee and frying bacon filled the air. She moved about the room with all the confidence of a fully sighted person.

'Banyon's men are back again,' she said, suddenly.

Brad followed her to the door and looked out. Down beside the creek, two men were busy replacing the wire in the broken fence. A bale of barb-wire was strapped to a mule. Brad fastened his Peacemaker about his waist. He flipped the weapon out and checked the loads.

'Lisa, you stay right here and keep outa sight.'

He put on his Stetson and stepped outside. The early-morning air was fresh and clear. As he approached the creek, the two men continued with their task unaware of his approach.

A dozen paces away, it finally registered. One of the men whirled round.

'What the hell!' he exclaimed.

His hand strayed to the gun strapped

to his hip, but he thought the better of it when he saw Brad's Peacemaker was already trained on him.

'I take it you two are workin' for Judge Banyon?' Brad enquired as he drew closer.

'And who might you be?' one of the men demanded.

'I'm askin' the questions. Why you are doing this?'

The men looked shiftily at each other. 'The judge's orders,' one of them said. 'He told us to fix this broken fence.'

'I wonder why? Did he figure that the Warrenders would have no further use for passin' this way?'

The two men exchanged uneasy glances.

Brad raised his gun and cocked it. 'Boys, my temper's on a short fuse. Late yesterday I done buried three members of the Warrender family. Somebody strung 'em up and the way I'm feeling is that iffen I don't get me some straight answers I'm gonna be burying two more.'

'We don't know nuthin' about it, mister,' one of the men growled. 'We're just a coupla hired hands.'

'Well, in that case, maybe you won't mind cutting me a way through that fence.'

'Mister, we'll be plumb out of a job if we don't do what the boss says.'

'Better be out of a job than dead,' Brad said harshly. 'Now you best start cuttin' that wire or I'll be puttin' holes in the pair of you.'

'You wouldn't do that,' one of the men said incredulously.

'Try me. No one showed any mercy to the Warrenders. For all I know you were part of the gang that murdered them.'

'Best do as he says, Red,' one of the men said reluctantly.

'We ain't got no choice,' his companion grumbled.

When they had finished, Brad said. 'OK, now get the hell outa here.'

'If I was you, mister, I'd stay outa

this,' one of the men said. 'The boss ain't a man to mess with.'

Brad waited until the men disappeared over the rise and then returned to the house.

'We'd best get movin', Lisa,' he said.

'Banyon won't do anything now,' she replied. 'We're out of here and that's all he cares about.'

They breakfasted on bacon, eggs and coffee. As they prepared to leave, Brad noticed the girl was wearing a riding habit.

'Can you ride?' he enquired.

'Of course,' came the reply. 'But they stole my pony along with the other stock.'

'Iffen I'd realized, I'd have taken one of those men's hosses from them just now,' Brad said.

'I'm glad you didn't. That would have made you a horse-thief. Pa always said you don't come lower than a horse-thief. I'll ride your horse with you.'

Brad saddled up Blaze and took the girl up. They left the farm the way they had come, passing through the newly created gap in the wire, across the creek, following the way which led to the main trail to Paradise.

They hit the trail without incident, but further along, Brad became aware of activity ahead. Drawing nearer, he soon saw that a group of men were working on a line of fencing. As he drew closer he saw that they were hammering in posts to carry the fence straight across the line of the trail he was following.

'This is just plumb loco,' he muttered.

There were five of them, all wearing leather gloves to enable them to handle the gleaming strand of barb-wire they were drawing off a wooden reel mounted on an axle on the wagon-bed. The legend WASHBURN & MOEN, the name of the largest manufacturer and supplier of barb-wire in the country, was stamped in bold black letters on the side of the reel.

'Howdy,' Brad said, drawing Blaze to a halt.

In response, a man stepped forward from behind the wagon. Brad had his measure immediately. He was a big bull of a man with blond hair. Toting a gun, he had the air of one used to being obeyed — instantly.

'You the boss round here?' Brad enquired.

'Right first time, mister. I'm Jess Collier. Judge Banyon's top-screw. If you're lookin' fer a job, there ain't none. So just keep movin', that's my best advice.'

'I believe this is the way to Paradise,' Brad said evenly.

Collier guffawed.

'Who's askin'?' he demanded.

'Name's Rio — Frank Rio. Now, are you gonna let us through that wire?'

'Maybe yesterday,' Collier said. 'But not today, not any more.'

'So how are we gonna get into town, iffen you don't mind me askin'?' Brad demanded.

'Mister. I do mind. So do me a favour. Turn your hoss round and get the hell outa here.'

'Well, now, I guess that ain't bein' very helpful,' Brad drawled. 'I got me some business to do in Paradise. Now cut that wire and unblock this road.'

As his voice rose in exasperation, the hammering stopped and one by one, the men at work stopped and stared at him, their hostility evident in the expressions even though their faces were caked with dust and sweat.

'You got tired of livin', mister?' one of them said.

Brad had already noticed that despite their toil, not one man had discarded his gun belt.

'Now for the last time, Mr Rio, turn that hoss about and get the hell outa here before I shoot your ass off,' Collier said.

Brad took control over the feeling of exasperation building up inside him. He'd lost count of the number of times he'd been confronted with blustering bullies like this. To Collier's vast surprise, he dismounted and walked over to him.

'Listen, Collier, I don't take no shit from meat-heads like you,' he said, keeping his voice low so that the girl wouldn't hear. 'Now are you gonna open that trail or do I have to shut your big mouth?'

Collier stared at him, completely taken aback.

'You're a windbag, Collier,' Brad went on. 'You like dishin' it out, but when it comes to takin' it, you're like all the rest, scared witless when someone calls your bluff.'

'Now wait a minute.'

The men behind Collier must have heard every word of the exchange, but he was spared further embarrassment by the sound of riders approaching.

Seconds later, three men reined in their horses to a halt.

'Somethin' ailing you here, Jess?' one of the newcomers, whom Brad took to be their leader, said. He was clean-shaven except for a black moustache. His long black, travel-stained coat was unbuttoned, revealing a pair of pearl-handled revolvers. But what distinguished them most were the badges they were sporting prominently on their lapels — the five-pointed Lone Star worn by the Texas Rangers.

'Ain't nuthin' I can't handle,' Collier muttered.

With the arrival of the newcomers, Brad realized he'd lost the initiative. Lisa's safety was paramount.

'I'm takin' this young lady to her grandparents in Paradise,' he explained. 'All I'm askin' for is free passage along the trail.'

'And I just done told him it ain't no public highway no more, Captain Tait,' Collier said to the leader of the newcomers. 'He has to make a detour to get to Paradise.'

'How far?' Brad demanded.

'Oh, about three hours' ride. I guess.'

'Is this some kinda joke?' Brad demanded. He looked at the leader of the three riders. 'You're Rangers, how can you allow this to happen?' he demanded.

'Guess there ain't nuthin' we can do about it, mister,' came the reply. 'Judge

Banyon's got legal entitlement to this land. He's within his rights to fence it.'

'But . . . '

The confrontation was interrupted by the sound of an approaching buckboard. It was being driven at a furious pace along the trail Brad had just followed. He had a bad moment when he figured the driver hadn't seen the wire fence blocking the road and was relieved when the buckboard pulled up just short of it.

Brad was amazed when he saw that the suicidal driver was a young woman. Freckle-faced, the wayward strands of her corn-yellow hair were barely concealed by a Stetson.

'Cut this goddamn wire — I gotta get through to Paradise,' she shouted. 'I need the doctor, my pa's fallen off his hoss and hurt his back.'

'You ain't goin' nowhere,' Collier replied harshly. 'You nesters'll make up any excuse to go where you're not wanted.'

'It's not like that!' the young woman

cried. 'I've told you, my pa needs medical attention urgently.'

'You heard the young lady,' Brad said.

'I just done told you. Turn around and go back the way you came,' Jess Collier said harshly.

'I don't think so,' Brad said.

'You reckon?'

Jess Collier's face broke into a triumphant grin as Brad found himself facing his drawn gun.

Collier sniggered. 'Now mister, I suggest you turn around and leave this county, pronto,' he said.

'But what about my pa?' The young woman's face was distraught.

Brad turned slowly round, deliberately ignoring the gunmen.

'Get the hell outa here, while you're still alive,' Collier snarled.

'Throw that gun down or I'll blow your head off.'

Brad half turned to see the young woman standing on the buckboard. She was holding a double-barrelled shotgun and the barrel was pointing unwaveringly at Collier.

'What's with you? Are you crazy?' Collier demanded.

'Do as I say!'

There was no mistaking the urgency in the young woman's voice.

Brad had seen many acts of courage in his time, but this took some beating. He hadn't the slightest doubt she meant what she said. His own Peacemaker added the decisive factor to the tense situation.

'I guess you best do as the young lady says,' Captain Tait advised.

As Collier dropped his gun, one of his men went to the wagon, picked up a pair of wire-cutters and set about cutting the taut strands. When the way was clear, without another word, the young woman took up the reins and urged her horse through the gap.

'Lucky for you, Rio,' Collier said to Brad with contempt. 'You won't always have a woman to back you.'

'Do you know who she is?' Brad

asked Lisa as they followed the buckboard.

'Yes, her name is Charlie Lister. Her family run a farm at Yellow Springs. It's about an hour's ride east from ours.'

They caught up with the buckboard after about a mile. Brad moved over to one side to avoid the cloud of dust behind it.

'Are them Rangers followin' us?' the young woman demanded.

'As it happens, no,' Brad replied. 'That was a very foolish thing to do back there, Charlie, but thanks all the same.'

'Guess I was desperate,' she replied. 'I meant it, you know. I would have pulled the trigger if he hadn't cut that wire.'

'I believe you,' Brad said. 'And I guess them Rangers did, too.'

'You want me to take Lisa on board?' Charlie enquired.

'I guess it'll be a mite more comfortable for her iffen you do,' Brad replied.

'Mr Rio is taking me to my grandfather's place in town,' Lisa said as they paused to make the exchange.

Noting Charlie's puzzled expression, Brad added, 'Lisa's folks were murdered yesterday by a gang of men. Lisa survived only because she hid in a barn.'

Charlie was horrified. 'Hell, I never thought it would come to this!' she exclaimed.

'When we get into town, you go fetch the doctor,' Brad said. 'I'll leave Lisa with her grandfather. I'll have a word with the sheriff. After that, I'll ride back home with you.'

'I'd appreciate it if you would,' Charlie replied. 'I sure don't fancy another run-in with those guys. Next time I may not get so lucky.'

Brad dropped back as the trail narrowed and the outskirts of what he surmised must be Paradise came into view. Charlie took a side turning off the main street, leaving him to take Lisa on board again and ride past a line of

clapboard buildings with raised sidewalks. Further along the buildings
became more substantial, culminating
in a bank built with an elegant stone
façade.

'Look out for a hardware store with
the name of Jacob Warrender, Mr Rio,'
Lisa said. 'It's on the main street just
beyond the centre.'

Their passage elicited curious glances
from the passers-by. Brad found the
store without any difficulty. He dismounted, helped the girl down and she
hung on to his arm negotiating the
steps faultlessly as he led her up the
steps on to the sidewalk. The store was
empty apart from an old-timer with a
snow-white beard of biblical proportions standing behind the counter.

'Howdy, what can I do for you,' the
old-timer greeted him with a friendly
smile. His expression changed when he
saw the girl.

'Why Lisa, what brings you here?'

'Oh Grandpa . . . '

As Lisa broke down in tears, her

grandfather opened the counter-hatch and rushed to comfort her.

'What's happened?' he demanded of Brad. 'I've never seen her like this before. Just who are you, mister?'

He listened in mounting anger as Brad answered his questions, taking care to keep his identity secret.

'If you will take care of Lisa, I gotta go and see the sheriff,' he concluded.

'I wish you joy of him,' Jacob muttered. 'I guess he knows which side his bread is buttered. And from what I can see, the cattlemen have gotten the Rangers eating outa their hands, too.'

'One thing more,' Brad said. 'I'd like to purchase a set of wire-cutters from you.'

The old man looked at him curiously. 'I take it you know what's goin' on round here?'

Brad nodded.

'Gimme a minute,' the old man said.

He disappeared into the back of his shop. He returned a few minutes later.

'Here you are.' He handed Brad the

tool as he spoke. 'No, I won't take anythin'. But I should watch your step, mister, if I was you, the stakes have been raised now the Rangers are here.'

As Brad took his leave, he called after him, 'Thanks for taking care of my granddaughter, Mr Rio. And for Pete's sake watch your back.'

Brad was just about to mount Blaze when the door of the store opened behind him and Lisa appeared.

'Mr Rio,' she called out. 'There is something I want to tell you.' A shaft of sunlight highlighted her sightless eyes as she spoke.

'Why, what is it, Lisa?'

He strode back up the steps and on to the side-walk as he spoke.

'I believe you are a lawman.'

Brad glanced sharply at her, but her sightless eyes told him nothing. 'What makes you think that?'

'It's the way you keep on asking questions.'

'OK — I'm a Texas Ranger,' he conceded. 'But I'm travellin' incognito.

I'd be obliged if you would tell nobody — not even your grandparents.'

'So your name isn't Frank Rio?'

'I guess not, but I'd rather keep the real one to myself for the time being.'

The girl nodded. 'You didn't recognize Captain Tait.'

A bald statement of fact, not a question.

Brad shook his head in wonderment at the girl's remarkable intuition.

'Never saw him before in my life. But then again, there's plenty of Rangers I've never met. You got somethin' on your mind?'

The girl nodded. 'I'm confused. Captain Tait and his men are the ones who came to the farm.'

'You sure about that, Lisa?' Brad demanded.

'Please understand,' the girl replied, 'I may not be able to see but I can hear as well as anyone. I'll remember that man's voice, and those of his companions, for the rest of my life.'

3

'Well, what is it?' Judge Banyon snapped.

Jess Collier fiddled with his hat. 'Sir, I guess we got us a problem.'

Banyon leaned back in his chair and regarded his foreman over the half-moon lenses of his wire-framed spectacles. It gave him a curiously academic look.

'I done sent two of the boys to mend the fence down at the Warrenders' place,' Collier continued.

'Go on.'

Collier gave a nervous cough. He had thought very carefully about what he was going to say. But under the steely gaze of his boss, that was easier said than done.

'Well, they met up with this guy and, well, I guess he kinda stopped them.'

'They met up with this guy and you guess he kinda stopped them?' mimicked Banyon. 'What the hell do you mean by that?'

Collier felt his buttocks clench involuntarily. Banyon had been one hell of a slave-driver in the army. If he found out about the humiliating incident with the Lister girl there would be hell to pay.

'Well?'

'I guess they didn't have no choice,' Collier replied. 'He got the drop on them and ordered them off.'

Banyon stared at him. 'Who was he?'

'They ain't never seen him before. Says his name is Frank Rio. I checked out the Warrenders' place for myself later. The place is deserted. I found three fresh graves round the back of the house. Tait's done the job, OK. I reckon that guy Rio must have buried them.'

'Three, you say? The Warrenders were a family of four. So who did they miss?'

Collier bit his lip. The significance of the girl's presence had eluded him in the heat of his confrontation with the stranger.

Banyon subsided back into his chair and Collier spent an uncomfortable two minutes that seemed like an hour as his employer sat deep in thought.

'Right,' Banyon said abruptly, 'I want every fence that has been cut replaced.'

'What about this stranger?'

'I want him out of this,' Banyon snapped.

Collier licked his lips nervously. The humiliation he had endured still rankled with him. He had lost face and the need to gain revenge and reestablish his standing in the eyes of his men was burning him up. He needed to act quickly. The thought of killing a man never usually troubled him but this guy, he had to admit, was different. In the confrontation back on the trail he had shown a fearlessness bordering on contempt. Without the Lister girl's intervention, Tait and his men would have had to gun him down to stop him.

'How do we do it?' he enquired.

'That isn't your problem. You just go and fix the wire.'

* ★ ★

Sheriff Lee Rance was sitting at his desk when Brad knocked and entered his office. An albino, Rance's beautifully waved hair, spotlessly white shirt, embroidered vest and immaculately tailored grey suit didn't impress Brad. His soft, damp, flaccid handshake did nothing to change Brad's opinion that he was a dudie.

'What brings you here, Mr Rio?' Rance enquired affably after the opening pleasantries had been exchanged.

'I'm just passin' through,' Brad told him. 'Been working in the Nueces Valley. I'm heading north to see my folks.'

Vance listened while Brad recounted what had happened to the Warrenders.

'His daughter tells me that Judge Banyon was harrying him off his land,' he concluded.

'Now wait a minute,' Rance said. 'I guess you've only heard one side of the story. There are three major landowners in this county, Judge Banyon, Mayor Cowper and Mr Fife, who manages a spread for a foreign-based conpany. These people have invested a great deal of time, money and effort to establish themselves. You can't blame them for defending themselves when a bunch of Johnny-come-latelies try to muscle in on their land.'

'I wouldn't have thought such people had any muscle,' Brad pointed out.

'Individually, they don't,' the sheriff admitted. 'But collectively they can make their presence felt in no uncertain way. In some areas, fences have been systematically cut almost as fast as they have been erected.'

'That's hardly surprising, if the fences bar access to water and public rights of way. Fencing off the open range was always gonna cause trouble.'

The sheriff smiled. 'Spoken like an old-time cowman, Mr Rio. Times are changing. If the cattle industry is to survive, the land must be fenced. Barb-wire takes no room. You don't have to wait for it to grow and it doesn't exhaust the soil like the Osage hedges they tried. It casts no shade and it's proof against high winds. Snow doesn't drift against it. It's durable and above all, it's cheap.'

'Spare me the lecture,' Brad snapped. 'We're dealin' with a human problem as well.'

Rance sighed. He glanced down at his beautifully manicured nails. 'I did advise the cattlemen not to take the law into their own hands, but when you consider the provocation they have endured from men like Bill Warrender, I must say I can hardly blame them for bringing in the Rangers.'

'And how do you feel about the Rangers coming in to do the cattlemen's dirty work?'

'I don't think anything.'

'How do you explain what has happened to the Warrenders?'

Rance shrugged. 'You tell me, Mr Rio. This is the West. Life is cheap. People get themselves killed for very little reason.'

'How about you ride over and take a look?'

'What good would that do? The Rangers are in charge here now. The men who did it will be long gone. Look, Mr Rio, I understand your concern, but you know how it is. My advice is don't get involved.'

Brad had heard quite enough from this self-satisfied sonofabitch. Clearly he was in the vest-pockets of the cattlemen, a puppet saying and doing exactly what he was told.

He said, 'Well, if you want to talk to Lisa, she is staying with her grandparents.'

'I believe the girl is blind,' Rance replied. 'So she won't be of any help.' He looked at Brad curiously. 'What's your interest in this anyway?'

'I found her wanderin' loose on the range,' Brad replied as he walked towards the door. 'I couldn't just walk away and leave her.'

Charlie was waiting for him when he left the office. She was standing beside the buckboard. When he saw the anger in her face, he said:

'Why, what's the matter, I thought you was fetchin' the doctor?'

'He's drunk. I can't get any sense out of him nohow.'

'We'll see about that,' Brad said grimly. He unhitched Blaze and swung into the saddle. 'Take me round to his house.'

Charlie sprang into the driving-seat of the buckboard and Brad followed her back along the main street until he turned right into a road of private dwellings.

'You stay here,' he ordered, when she indicated the house. 'What's his name?'

'Logan,' came the reply.

Brad strode up the path and subjected the front door to a thunderous knocking.

'Go away,' a slurred voice shouted from within.

'Open up,' Brad replied. 'Otherwise I'm gonna break down the door.'

After a few seconds pause, there was

the grate of a bolt being drawn and the door opened.

Brad was used to seeing many strange sights, but he was totally unprepared for that of the baggy-eyed, pot-bellied apology for a man who stood swaying in the doorway.

'See what I mean?' Charlie called out. 'When he's sober, Pa reckons he's the finest medic this side of Austin.'

'Is that so? Then I guess we'd best get him back into shape. You go find his bag, it must be somewhere in the house.'

In his drunken state Dr Logan was in no position to resist as Brad pounced on him and dragged him by the scruff of his neck the length of the street until he came to a water trough. Once there, before a crowd of amused onlookers, Brad dunked him bodily into it.

The doctor floundered for a few seconds before he surfaced, spouting a stream of curses.

Charlie appeared with the buckboard.

'I got me his bag!' She held it up in both hands triumphantly.

'OK,' Brad replied. He hauled the doctor out of the trough. Charlie dropped the tailgate of the buckboard and, grasping the doctor by his collar and the seat of his pants, Brad heaved him straight into it. He picked up the bag and tossed it after him.

'Now let's leave this goddamn place before I explode,' he said.

'Hope you haven't hurt him,' Charlie remarked as they left town.

'You gotta be jokin',' Brad said. 'Guys like him are tougher'n old boots.'

Which sentiment was reinforced when an hour later, the doctor's head popped over the side of the buckboard.

'Excuse me, old boy, would you mind telling me where I am?' he enquired of Brad who was cantering alongside.

Brad stared at him. 'You from England?'

'Of course,' came the reply. 'I was born in Sussex, old boy. Educated at Eton and Oxford.'

Brad had never heard of any such places, so he wasn't impressed.

'Would you mind awfully if I enquired where we're going?'

Brad shook his head in amazement. 'Charlie Lister's father has had an accident,' he said. 'He reckons you're the man we need to put him right.'

'Well, I did dabble a little in medicine in my younger days. Never took a degree, though. Woman trouble, old boy. My professor's wife to be precise. A lovely, voluptuous woman with an insatiable passion for me. Her hubby caught us *in flagrante delicto*. Had to fork the saddle in a hurry and get out of town pronto, as you Westerners say. That's why I'm here in Texas. Now tell me, please, where are we going?'

Brad started to explain, but before he had finished, he was interrupted by loud snores.

'I hope this guy's worth all the trouble we've gone to,' Brad remarked to Charlie.

'He's all we've got, I guess,' she replied.

They came to the place that had been fenced off and Brad's expression became grim when he saw the wire had been replaced. Had the way been left clear, he might have been persuaded that his presence had redressed the balance of the situation, but now he knew it hadn't. All his experience told him that from now on, things would only get worse before they got better.

'What do we do now?' Charlie enquired.

He fished out the wirecutters. 'I got me these back in Paradise,' he said. 'Lisa's grandpa gave 'em to me. Figured I might have use fer 'em.'

'Thank God!' Charlie exclaimed. 'I guess I'll just stretch my legs.' She dismounted from the buckboard as Brad set to work on the fence.

As the first length of wire recoiled Brad detected a movement out of the corner of his eye. A lifetime of living with the threat of danger triggered a reaction in him with the sensitivity of a hairspring.

'Get down!' He flung himself on Charlie, bore her to the ground and rolled her over and over under the buckboard.

The air around them was full of whining lead as they came under attack.

Pushing Charlie to one side, Brad drew out his Peacemaker and emptied it, firing blindly in the direction he figured the bullets were coming from.

As he paused to reload, he became aware that the firing had ceased. He crawled forward to investigate. When no more shots came, he turned back to Charlie.

'You OK?'

She nodded, too shocked to speak.

Cautiously, Brad peered round the wheel of the buckboard. Whoever was out there could be playing cat to his mouse, waiting for him to show before pumping him full of lead.

He waited.

After five minutes, Charlie said, 'It

looks like we're trapped, Mr Rio. What are we gonna do?'

For answer, Brad eased further forward until he was beyond the shelter of the buckboard. The vehicle hadn't moved. He figured he knew why. Still no sound except, to his intense relief, that of Blaze snorting gently a few yards away.

Slowly, very slowly, he rose to a standing position, holding his Peacemaker cocked, ready to sell his life dearly if necessary.

Nothing happened. Not an insect stirred in the wilderness surrounding the trail. A buzzard sailed serenely against a backdrop of fluffy white clouds in a sky of azure blue as it slowly turned through a full circle.

He took a few steps forward and glanced back, still vigilant. His reasoning as to why the buckboard hadn't moved was verified. The horse lay dead in its traces.

His low whistle brought Blaze trotting over to him.

'Is it OK for me to come out?'

Charlie's query made him jump. With an effort, he pulled himself together.

'Is the doctor OK?'

Brad was suddenly overwhelmed with a sense of foreboding. His nerves were as taut as the wires still blocking the road.

'You OK?' Charlie asked.

He nodded. Mounting the step of the buckboard, he looked down into the well. The doctor lay sprawled on his back, arms akimbo, his face twisted into the all-too-familiar rictus of death. The hole in his forehead told its own story. When the shooting started, he must have looked over the side of the buckboard and been killed instantly.

Charlie gasped.

'Oh no!' she exclaimed, her eyes wide with horror.

Brad experienced a feeling of helplessness, the like of which he hadn't felt for a long time.

'There isn't another doctor in the county,' Charlie said bleakly.

The girl's despair reawakened the resolve in Brad. He had faced similar demands before and risen to them. Now he would have to do it again, no matter what the cost. Confronted by ruthless men, he would have to match their ruthlessness with a determination that exceeded theirs.

'Stay here,' he ordered. 'Keep down by the wheel outa sight.'

Charlie obeyed him without question. He left her and advanced, gun in hand, crossing the trail into the fringe of the wilderness that had concealed his attackers.

Senses honed by years of experience, he soon formed a picture of what had happened.

'Well?' Charlie enquired, when he returned.

'All the sign shows there was only one man.' Brad held up a spent cartridge. 'He was firing a rifle. I reckon I must have got lucky and hit him. He lost some blood before he got away.'

'So at least we are safe,' Charlie said.

'For the moment,' Brad agreed. 'I guess we'd best get to your place. My hoss ain't accustomed to being in harness, so let's leave the buckboard and push on. He can carry the two of us.'

'What about Doctor Logan? We can't just leave him here like this.'

Brad agreed. He dropped the tailgate of the buckboard, lifted out the corpse and dragged it out on to the trail.

'Help me find some rocks to cover him,' he said to Charlie. 'I'll fix for him to get a decent burial later.'

When their task was completed, Brad took Charlie up behind him and rode the last ten miles to Yellow Springs.

From a slight rise in the trail he reined in to look down on a sod-roofed house similar to the one inhabited by the Warrenders. It was supplied with water by the lower reaches of the same creek.

'What are we gonna tell Ma?'

Charlie looked at Brad with big round eyes. In contrast to Lisa's

65

sightless stare they were full of apprehension.

'Best leave it to me,' he said.

He eased Blaze down the gentle slope towards the cabin. The barking of a large dog heralded their approach. As they dismounted, a big, robust woman of around forty appeared in the doorway.

'You took your time,' the woman said to Charlie. She stared at Brad. 'Who are you, mister? Where is Doctor Logan?'

She listened in silence as Brad explained what had happened.

'How is Pa?' Charlie enquired as they went inside the cabin.

'He's no worse. It's his back. I don't think he's broken anything, thank God. Thanks for bringing Charlie home, Mr Rio,' she said to Brad as they walked to the bed on which the injured man was lying. His head was wrapped in a bloodstained bandage.

'Joe, you got a visitor,' she said.

The man smiled wanly. He was obviously in pain.

'I guess there's not a lot Doctor Logan could do if he was here,' Mrs Lister remarked. 'These things take their own time, I guess.'

The resignation in her remark reflected Brad's thoughts precisely. Right now what concerned him was the bloody furrow across the back of the man's right hand.

'What are we going to do, Ma?' Charlie enquired anxiously.

'What are we gonna do?' her mother echoed. 'Why, I guess we're gonna stay right here and manage as best we can.'

4

At Mrs Lister's insistence, Brad bunked down in the cabin for the night. But his sleep was troubled by thoughts of Lisa Warrender's revelation. If she was right about Tait, then he and his men couldn't be Texas Rangers. That meant they must be outlaws masquerading under the badge. He had never heard of Tait; it was more than likely the name was an alias and Brad had no knowledge of the outlaws in this part of Texas. Maybe the girl was wrong, but he had a gut feeling she wasn't. Thing was, how to prove she was right?

'Pa ain't in such pain,' Charlie had reported, 'but he's findin' it hard to move.'

Brad marvelled at the fortitude of Western womenfolk.

He rose and by the time he went outside to sluice his face at the pump the sun had risen over the horizon, flooding the prairie with golden light. He removed his shirt and the chill of the water revived his flagging spirits. The smell of coffee sharpened his appetite. He stood for a moment, collecting his thoughts, trying to form some kind of plan to resolve the problems facing him.

He was so absorbed he was unaware of Charlie's presence until she said:

'You look like a guy with things on his mind, Mr Rio.'

'For Pete's sake, call me Frank,' he said.

'OK. Pete — Frank.' She looked at him with an expression a mixture of amusement and curiosity. Her blue eyes dropped to view his slab-muscled upper torso with unashamed interest. 'You don't have to concern yourself any more with us now, Frank. You've done enough and we're very grateful to you.'

Brad pulled on his shirt. 'Does your pa know what happened to the Warrenders?'

She shook her head. 'I told ma but we haven't told him yet.'

Before Brad could say more, the drumming of hoofs attracted their attention. They turned to see a bunch of a dozen men splashing through the creek.

'Banyon,' Lisa muttered as the riders drew up their horses in front of the house, their mounts blowing and snorting. The leader drew slightly ahead of them. Brad noticed that neither Jess Collier nor Tait and his men were present.

Banyon removed his hat. 'Sorry to hear about your husband's accident, Mrs Lister,' he said. 'I stopped by to see if there was anything I could do.'

'We don't need no help from you,' Mrs Lister snapped.

'Is that so?' Banyon's eyes settled on Brad. 'You must be the guy who prevented my men from going about their lawful business yesterday.'

'Since when has the law authorized fencing-off trails people have always used?' Brad retorted.

'They have no right to cross my land,' Banyon said. 'I have all the plans and documents to prove that I am acting within my rights. And, what's more, the Rangers are here now to enforce it.'

'And do these rights extend to driving people away from their farms?'

'Now wait a minute,' Banyon shot back. 'I'm not answerable to you.'

'Why have you come here?' Mrs Lister demanded.

'When I heard about your husband's accident I figured you'd be in trouble. I came to make you an offer for the farm.'

'Get the hell outa here, Banyon,' a voice roared behind them.

Everyone's attention focused on Joe Lister. He pushed his wife to one side and, lurching unsteadily on his feet as though he was drunk, his face contorted with pain, he confronted Banyon and his men.

Banyon leaned forward in his saddle.

'Face it, Lister, you and your kind are finished here. Best you sell up while you got the chance and go back East where you belong.'

'No damned bluebelly ever gives me orders,' Joe Lister snarled. 'Like I said, get off my property.'

Almost too late, Brad saw Joe's right arm come up, his hand holding a gun. Quick as a flash, Brad took a step forward and snatched it from him.

'What the hell are you playin' at?' Joe demanded.

'I guess he just did you a favour,' Banyon said. 'Now I'm a reasonable man, Lister. I'll give you a week to take up my offer.'

'And then what?' Brad demanded.

'Don't worry, he'll sell.'

'That's where you're wrong,' Mrs Lister replied, defiance glittering in her eyes. 'Ain't no question of us sellin' out. This is the only place we've ever had. We're stayin' right here.'

Banyon replaced his hat. 'I admire your pluck, ma'am. I understand you must be upset. But, like I said, we'll talk again in the not too distant future.'

As Banyon made to leave, Brad said, 'I might just mention that I don't take kindly to being bushwhacked.'

Banyon stared at him. 'What are you talking about?'

'Me and Charlie rode into town to fetch the doctor. We was bushwhacked on the way back where the wire crossed the trail. Dr Logan is dead.'

Banyon's grip on his reins tightened until his knuckles showed white. 'I don't know anything about this,' he muttered.

'Why, you do surprise me,' Brad drawled. 'Bein' as you claim the land where we were attacked belongs to you.'

'I can't be everywhere,' Banyon snapped.

'I ain't been a day in this county,' Brad said, 'and already I've seen four murders.'

'So what's it to you?' Banyon demanded. 'Captain Tait and his men are investigating.'

Brad watched as Banyon wheeled his horse round; the accompanying riders parted to let him through and then closed in again behind him, following his lead back the way they had come.

'I get the feelin' Judge Banyon didn't get what he came for,' Charlie remarked. She glanced admiringly at Brad, 'It would have been a different story if you hadn't been here, I guess.'

'That man is bad,' Joe Lister said as Brad helped him back into the house. 'All bluebellies is bad.'

'Maybe,' Brad replied. 'But the war's long over.'

Once he was settled on his bed, Joe regarded Brad curiously.

'So were you in the war, Frank?'

'I was just a kid,' Brad replied. 'I ran away from home. Rode as a trooper with Jeb Stuart until he was killed.'

'I guess you saw some action, then?'

'It's in the past,' Brad said. 'The next generation is sick of hearin' about it.'

'You're dead right,' Charlie said. 'All Pa ever does is go on about the war.

74

Anyone would think it's the only thing that happened in his life.'

'Hush your mouth!' her mother scolded her. She turned to Brad. 'Don't let us keep you, Mr Rio. You've done more than enough and we're obliged to you for that. Now, let me cook breakfast for you before you leave. Come and help me, Charlie.'

'So they've brought in the Rangers!' Joe exclaimed when the womenfolk had left. 'They will back the landowners, that's certain. We ain't gotta chance now they're here.'

'What makes you say that?' Brad asked.

'Because the law is always on the side of the rich and powerful.'

Brad winced inwardly. He fished out the makings and rolled a cigarette. He offered it to Joe, but he refused.

'You didn't just happen an accident, did you?'

Joe stared at Brad. 'What are you talkin' about?'

'You don't get marks like that by

fallin' off a hoss,' Brad said. He indicated the long furrow across the back of the other man's right hand as he spoke.

'Meanin' what?'

'Well, you and I, being both ex-army men, I reckon we both know a bullet graze when we see one.'

Joe turned his head to one side and said nothing.

'How about you level with me?' Brad went on. 'OK, let me guess. Somebody bushwhacked you. The bullet winged you. Your hoss spooked and threw you. They left you fer dead.'

'I guess that's about the size of it,' Joe agreed grudgingly.

'It don't take a genius to figure that the man behind it is Banyon. He won't do his own dirty work, that's fer sure.'

Joe stared at Brad. 'You seem to know all the answers, mister.'

'Assuming Banyon is behind all this, what I don't understand is why the Warrenders were massacred and you and your family weren't.'

'Bill Warrender was our leader. I was his *segundo*. Along with Jake Griffin from Owl Creek, there's a score of us altogether. With him and me outa the way, they figured they'd frighten the rest off. I guess I didn't like to tell my family about my bein' shot at — I didn't want to scare 'em.'

'You'd best tell me the full story,' Brad said.

'The big cattlemen in this county want every last acre. They'll stop at nothing to make sure they get 'em. Even to fencing off roads and water. And Banyon's made damn sure they've got the law on their side — every time they are challenged they wave a piece of paper at you. Bill, Jake Griffin from Owl Creek and me decided to give 'em a run fer their money. Every time they put up a fence against us, we cut it. The others joined us when they saw it was rilin' the cattlemen. We worked mostly at night, operatin' in pairs. It was like a game at first, but then the cattlemen turned nasty. Started makin' threats, said they'd bring the law in to deal with us — which is what they have done.'

Brad nodded thoughtfully.

Joe lifted himself on one elbow. 'You wouldn't be lookin' fer a job, by any chance, would you, Frank? I can't expect Charlie and her mother to run this place. I could pay thirty a month all-found.'

Brad resisted the temptation to succumb to his all too transparent plea for help.

'Sorry, Joe, I'm just passin' through. I'm on my way to see my folks up north.'

The early exertion had given Brad an appetite and he had no difficulty in consuming the steak and eggs Joe's wife prepared for him. Charlie was hungry, too, and matched him mouthful for mouthful.

'You movin' on?' she enquired as he poured a second mug of coffee.

'I guess so,' Brad replied.

'I been thinkin'. I believe the guy who bushwhacked us was Jess Collier,' Charlie said.

Brad stared at her. 'How did you figure that?' he demanded.

'Makes sense,' Charlie replied. 'He was in charge of Banyon's men fencing off the road. He didn't stop us gettin' through. I overheard what you said to him. You sure made him look small. I bet he hasn't told Banyon. He knows we would come back so he took the chance of bushwhacking you before you made any more trouble.'

'You could be right,' Brad mused.

'I must pick up the buckboard,' Charlie said. 'If you're headin' into town, can I ride with you?'

★ ★ ★

Banyon arrived back at his ranch in high dudgeon.

He dismounted, tossed the reins to a groom and strode into the house.

Once inside he went straight to the room at the back where Jess Collier lay on a bed, his face twisted in agony.

'What the hell is going on?' Banyon

79

demanded. 'You said you'd killed that stranger. I've just seen him at Yellow Springs as large as life.'

Beads of sweat stood out on Collier's face as he faced his angry boss.

'Jesus, I pumped enough lead at him to kill a reg'ment,' he said hoarsely. 'The bastard got lucky and hit me in the thigh. Did you get the doctor?'

'Logan is dead,' Banyon said harshly. 'We found him under some rocks beside the trail. He'd taken a bullet straight between the eyes. It looks like you shot the wrong man.' He eyed Collier balefully. 'I brought Captain Tait in to take care of things. What the hell's gotten into you? I employ you as a foreman, not as a gunman.'

Collier groaned. 'What am I gonna do? The lead's still in me. I need a doctor. If someone don't get it out soon, I could lose my leg.'

'You might even die,' Banyon said callously. 'Now Logan's dead, anything might happen.'

There was a tap on the door. Banyon opened it.

'Captain Tait's arrived. sir,' a cowhand reported.

* * *

Brad left the Listers with mixed feelings. It was going to be hard for them with Joe out of action, but he figured that as long as Banyon knew he was around they'd be safe.

He and Charlie arrived back at the place where they'd been bushwhacked and his lips tightened when he saw the trail had been fenced off yet again.

'Looks like they ain't gonna give up,' he muttered.

He dismounted and opened a gap again with the cutters to enable Charlie to retrieve the buckboard.

'By the way, thanks again fer helpin' us,' Charlie said as she made ready to leave.

'Can't say I did much,' Brad confessed.

'I dunno 'bout that. Just you bein' there did the trick as far as Banyon is concerned.' She took a step forward and kissed Brad on the cheek. She coloured slightly and took a step back. 'Gee, I'm sure as hell disappointed you didn't take up Pa's offer of a job. I guess Ma an' me can just about manage. And, I guess if there's Rangers around, we should be safe enough.'

Without waiting for Brad to reply, she sprang into the seat of the buckboard and gave her horse a light touch of the whip. Brad watched her leave until the buckboard was a cloud of dust on the horizon. He gave a wry smile. Maybe it was for the best. There was something about Charlie's undisguised admiration that could easily turn a man's head.

Turning back to the task in hand, Brad soon found the place where the attack had taken place. Following the day-old sign was a task which demanded the utmost concentration but to his immense satisfaction he tracked it back by a roundabout route until he reached a fenced-off area signed 'BAR B RANCH. PROP. JUDGE BANYON.

'Looks like you was right, Lisa,' he muttered.

Suddenly, he saw a clear picture of her face in his mind's eye and it troubled him. Just who was this man, Tait, and how had he come to be able to pull a trick like this?

★　★　★

'You took your time,' Banyon snapped as Aaron Tait sauntered into his office.

'Guess I ain't in the army no more, Major Banyon, sir,' Tait replied. He spat on the silver star pinned to his lapel and polished it briskly with the corner of a silk handkerchief.

Banyon winced inwardly. Once a keen and ambitious young officer, Tait's attitude and manners had deteriorated since they had last met. Like himself, he'd had a good education back East before the war. He could have done anything he wanted, but he had chosen to live outside the law.

Tait spat on his Ranger's badge and polished it between his finger and thumb.

'Say, I'm gettin' to quite like being a Ranger. I'm getting some respect at last. Nice place you got here.' He looked round as he spoke. 'Business is good, hey? You gotta be worth a few bucks I guess.'

Banyon made no comment. Despite Tait's lethargic nonchalance, he had the reputation of a ruthless gunman. Finding him and bringing him to Texas from his hideout in Arizona had been neither easy nor cheap.

Tait lounged against the wall, picking his teeth with a silver toothpick. He extracted a meaty tit-bit from a cavity, held it up to the light for a more thorough inspection and then flicked it away. By some strange quirk of vision, Banyon saw its trajectory through the air before it adhered itself to the wall.

'I'm not satisfied,' Banyon said. 'Joe Lister's still alive.'

Tait hitched his gunbelt with his thumbs. 'Is that so?'

'There's something else. Jess Collier tells me there are only three graves at the Warrenders' place. There should be four.'

'How come? Have you been checking up on me?'

With an effort, Banyon resisted the temptation to terminate the meeting right then. He had to remind himself that men like Tait didn't fight for causes any more, they sold their services to the highest bidder.

'When I pay good money, I expect to take delivery of the goods,' he said icily.

'I let Nat and Pete deal with Joe Lister,' Tait said. 'I'll talk to 'em.'

'Too late now, there's complications. We got a stranger in town, going under the name of Frank Rio. He seems mighty friendly with the nesters.'

'So I heard.'

Banyon stared at him. 'You know about him?'

'Sure do. Had the pleasure of meetin' him.'

'You gotta be jokin'.'

Banyon's eyes narrowed as he listened to Tait's version of the event involving Jess Collier.

'You'd better listen to what I have in mind,' Banyon said when Tait had finished. 'Although when you have, you might just want out of this.'

The piqued expression on Tait's face told Banyon he'd found his weak spot.

When Tait replied, 'Try me,' Banyon knew he had him hooked.

'Well, the way I see it,' Banyon went on, 'there's no evidence to pin anything on you about the Warrenders. In the circumstances, my priority now is to get rid of the Lister family. That didn't ought to be a problem, however; there's only one man standing in our way and that's this stranger. Now I got a strange feelin' about him.'

Tait's eyebrows rose.

'You figure he's a hired gun?'

'Either that, or more likely he's the law.'

'Jesus, you could be right!' Tait exclaimed. 'I've heard it said the Rangers sometimes operate incognito.'

'Well, I ain't taking any chances. There isn't room for both of you around here. I want you and your boys to take care of him.'

'How much?'

'A thousand.'

'Forget it.'

Tait was half-way to the door when Banyon said, 'Two thousand.'

'Four,' he said as Tait reached the door.

Tait hesitated, one hand on the knob.

'OK, four thousand. That's my limit. Half now, the other half when the job is done.'

Tait nodded.

Banyon went over to a safe and opened the door. He opened a cash box, counted out some greenbacks and handed them to Tait.

As the outlaw held out his hand,

Banyon said, 'On one condition.'

'What's that?'

'It's got to be done quickly. You're the organ-grinder so don't leave it to the monkeys this time. See to it personally. You understand?' He only just resisted the temptation to conclude with: 'That's an order.'

Tait's face broke into a gap-toothed smile.

'Consider it done Major Banyon — sir.'

5

Brad hurled away the dregs of coffee from his mug.

So what next?

The hell with it, Collier could wait. The amount of blood he'd lost he must be at death's door anyway. If Lisa was right, his main target had to be Tait. Only one thing bothered him; the guy must know by now that it was Lisa he had escorted to Paradise . . .

Suddenly he froze.

It had taken him for ever to realize Lisa was blind. It was odds-on Tait wouldn't know that either.

So if that fake Ranger had the sense he was born with, he must be wondering whether Lisa had witnessed the murder of her family at the farm.

Brad cursed himself roundly. Once Tait put two and two together, poor Lisa's life wouldn't be worth a candle.

He didn't have a moment to lose.

He swung easily into the saddle and headed towards Paradise.

★ ★ ★

'C'mon boys, we got things to do,' Tait said to his two *compadres*.

'Aye, aye, Captain,' Ned Dooley remarked with a wink. He was the oldest man of the three; a gash in his right cheek from his days in the Union Navy had disfigured his leathery features.

Pete Schulze's guffaw was cut short when Tait snapped, 'Don't you laugh too soon. You might be ridin' the range again sooner than you think.'

Dooley's jaw dropped. 'Why, boss?'

'Because we got us some opposition.'

'You mean that guy who faced down Collier at the fence?' Schulze demanded. Fresh-faced and with an incipient moustache, he was by far the youngest of the three. 'What was goin' on there?'

'I heard he started his own private war with Rio. Got his come-uppance apparently,' Dooley said with a snigger.

'Ferget it,' Tait snapped. 'It ain't important. It appears we missed someone when we hanged the Warrender family. The girl who was with Rio was the daughter. Banyon reckons he's either a hired gun or a lawman. He ain't sure which. Either way, Banyon's offerin' a big bounty iffen we kill him.'

'So we needn't worry about the girl?' Dooley remarked.

'Were you just born with a pea for a brain?' Tait said disgustedly. 'We can't take any chances. Suppose she was holed up someplace on the farm — if she saw us, she can testify against us. Before we deal with Rio, we have to find her and check out what she knows.'

'Jeeze, Aaron, you think of everythin'!' Schulze exclaimed.

'Good job I do,' Tait remarked. 'Or the pair of you would be rotting in jail by now. Let's ride into town.'

Two hours later, Tait and his men

rode into Paradise. They dismounted outside the sheriff's office. Tait led the way and opened the door without knocking.

'Why, Captain Tait, what can I do for you?' Rance said as they entered.

'Figure there's a stranger hereabouts,' Tait said. 'Name of Frank Rio. I need to question him about the Warrender murders.'

'Why, yes, that's so. He stopped by at the office yesterday to report that the Warrender family had been massacred. A matter with which I was already familiar.'

'Is that so? I believe he brought the Warrender kid into town with him.'

'So he did.'

'Where is he now?'

'I believe he was taking the doctor back to the Listers' place.'

'What did he do with the Warrender girl?'

'He left her with her grandfather. He runs the only hardware store in town. It's two blocks back. I guess you passed it on your way in. You can't miss it, it's got the Warrender name painted in big letters.'

When the door slammed shut, Rance sank back into his chair. Looking down, he was unnerved to see his hands were shaking. A professional card-player, Banyon had caught Rance using a Kepplinger Holdout to rig a poker game at the Cattlemen's Club. Banyon hadn't exposed him publicly, he had followed him to his room and forced him to reveal underneath his clothing the complex harness of pulleys, cords and telescoping silver-plated tubes hidden reaching from his forearm to his knees. It was the first and only time he had ever been caught out. Having to work to Judge Banyon's precise instructions was the price he had to pay for his silence.

★ ★ ★

Brad came to a running halt outside the hardware store. He flipped his horse's reins over the hitching rail and ran up the steps. Lisa's grandfather was serving a customer when he strode into the store.

'Sorry to interrupt,' Brad said. 'But I need to talk to you pronto, Mr Warrender.'

'Please excuse me for one moment, Mrs Fraser.' The storekeeper removed his wire-framed spectacles and regarded Brad with mild surprise.

'Can you tell me where I can find Lisa?' Brad demanded. 'I need to speak to her.'

★　★　★

Lisa was sitting in an upholstered chair in the parlour of her grandmother's house nursing the elbow she'd just hit on the sharp projection of an oak sideboard. The pain was enough to bring tears to her eyes, but she didn't complain. Trips and knocks were part and parcel of the blind person's lot in life and she had no mind to make a

94

fuss. Her grandma, Hester, was working in the kitchen preparing a meal and although she didn't feel particularly hungry, she took comfort from the familiar smell of beef and potatoes.

Somehow she could not get the man called Frank Rio out of her mind. She would never forget the patience and kindness he had shown her when he found her wandering on the prairie. She did not doubt for one moment that he was everything he said he was — and more. She recalled the stories Grandma Hester had read to her from a book called *Le Morte d'Arthur*. She smiled whimsically. Frank Rio was just like one of those ancient knights rescuing a damsel in distress . . .

She started as Tabby, the cat, rubbed her head against her bare foot. Reaching down, she forgot the pain in her elbow as she caressed the fur, sensing the vibration of Tabby's purring through her fingertips as she did so.

Her grandparents had listened to her account of what had happened back at the farm with unbelievable stoicism. Somehow she had drawn an inner strength from their mute acceptance of the tragedy. They were frontier people, used to hard knocks, not given to unbridled displays of grief.

'Hope them Rangers can find who did it,' was all her grandfather had said.

And this morning he had gone to the store at the behest of his wife, whom she had overheard saying:

'Jacob, the only way to cope with this sorrow is to work. We both know that.'

'But what's to become of Lisa?' the old man had said.

'It is early days yet. God will resolve it, all in His own good time,' came the reply.

The house was bigger than the soddy at Sandy Creek. Her father had always said that soon he would build as nice a house as his father had done. Built from timber it had a parlour and a kitchen with two rooms upstairs. The sound of approaching horses drew Lisa's attention and as her belief that the three riders were going to stop outside this house became reality, Lisa let Tabby go and moved cautiously back into the kitchen.

'We've got visitors, Grandma,' she said.

'Why, bless you, child, I never heard anyone. You must have a sixth sense,' Hester replied as a vigorous knocking started on the door. 'Who can it be?'

Lisa held back in the kitchen, straining every nerve to listen, whilst Hester went to answer it.

'Good morning to you, ma'am, I'm Captain Tait of the Rangers and I'm investigatin' the murders at Sandy Creek. I believe one child survived.'

'That's right. Frank Warrender was my son. Lisa, my granddaughter is right here with me.'

Lisa froze. It was that voice again, there was no mistaking it. The very sound of it revived all the horror of what had happened. She must get away . . .

'Please accept my condolences, Mrs

Warrender. I wonder if I might have a word with your granddaughter?'

'Why yes, of course. Lisa! Do come in.'

At this Lisa made a dash for the door, but she collided with the kitchen chair her grandmother had been sitting on. The chair fell over with a clatter and before she could reach the outer door, her grandmother said:

'Lisa, there's Captain Tait of the Rangers here. He wants to talk to you about what happened.'

Lisa fumbled for the chair, set it upright and with a fast beating heart she followed her grandmother back into the parlour. She was aware of the overwhelming presence of the man, she could smell the blend of sweat, both of man and horse mingled with stale tobacco.

'Now Lisa, why don't you tell Captain Tait what happened?' Hester coaxed her.

Lisa felt herself sway on her feet. Her worst fears had been realized sooner than she ever dreamed. She was overwhelmed with a sense of helplessness and terror.

'You must understand of course, Captain Tait, that Lisa is blind,' she heard her grandmother saying before Lisa fell heavily to the floor.

*   *   *

Brad reined in at the end of the road just in time to see three men dismounting outside the house that he realized was the one belonging to Lisa's grandparents. Only one man — that would be Tait — approached the door, the other two took out the makings and commenced rolling cigarettes.

Brad dismounted, drew Blaze back and tethered him to a hitching rail. Then he edged forward until he could see the house. Any moment now he expected to see Tait emerge with Lisa but he was surprised to see him come out alone. He made some remark to his companions that seemed to amuse them before all three mounted their horses and left.

Brad waited a few moments before he retrieved Blaze and approached the house.

A few more moments elapsed before Hester Warrender answered his knock. Her lined features took on an expression of relief when she recognized Brad.

'Please come in, Mr Rio,' she said. 'Lisa's had a nasty turn.'

Brad followed her through to the parlour where he found the girl sitting in a chair. As she turned her face towards him he saw her face was as pale as if she had seen a ghost.

'You OK, Lisa?' he enquired.

'Oh Mr Rio, thank goodness you've come,' she said with a sob.

'I'll go make some coffee,' her grandmother said.

'I just saw Tait and his men leaving,' Brad said gently when they were alone. 'What happened?'

Lisa reached out and gripped his

arm. 'He came here to get me, I know he did.'

'What makes you say that?' Brad asked gently.

Lisa raised her sightless eyes. They seemed to bore right through him.

'He didn't know I was blind at first. I pretended to faint when he started to ask questions. But then, whilst I was lying on the floor I heard him tell my grandma he wouldn't bother me any more because I couldn't have seen anything.' She clung to Brad with an intensity that almost unnerved him. 'Oh, Mr Rio, I'm frightened. Will you take me away from here?'

At that moment, Hester Warrender appeared in the doorway carrying a tray.

'Why, Lisa, what's this?' she exclaimed. She rounded on Brad. 'Why, Mr Rio, there ain't any call for you to take advantage of a young girl.'

'It isn't like that, Grandma,' the girl said, recovering her composure.

'Perhaps Mr Rio ought to tell you the truth.'

'I guess he'd better,' her grandmother replied testily.

Hester Warrender's expression became grave as Brad outlined his suspicion, based on Lisa's testimony, that Tait was an impostor.

'You sure about this?' she demanded of Lisa when Brad had finished.

The girl nodded.

'Do you believe her?' she asked Brad.

'I do,' Brad replied. 'But I guess I'm gonna need proof. Usually I would wire my HQ.'

Hester Warrender stared at him.

'Mr Rio is a Texas Ranger,' Lisa said quietly.

Before the woman could speak, Brad opened his jacket to reveal the badge that proclaimed his office.

'I often find it's best to go about incognito,' he told her.

'But that man Tait was openly wearing one of those!' Mrs Warrender exclaimed.

'They are easy enough to fake,' Brad said. 'But it's gonna be difficult to prove. Problem is I don't trust the sheriff. I believe he's in the pockets of the big cattlemen. I could wire my HQ in Austin, but I can't be sure the telegraph operator isn't in their pay as well.'

'Do you think Lisa is still in danger?'

Brad shook his head. 'I don't think so. I guess I'm gonna have to keep undercover for a while longer. Can I rely on you to keep quiet about this, Mrs Warrender?'

'What are you going to do? If Lisa is right, those evil men are capable of anything.'

'I'm frightened,' Lisa said. 'If they find out you are a Ranger they will kill you.'

'That's a risk I'll have to take, I guess,' Brad replied.

He left the Warrenders in a thoughtful mood. The only way to obtain verification of Tait's status was to ride on to the telegraph office at Truelove, the county seat of Logan a hundred miles further north. If he were to leave Paradise heading in that direction it would be consistent with what he had told people already. What worried him was the safety of the Lister family. Left to a man like Tait, the fate of Charlie and her mother didn't bear thinking about . . .

'Hey, mister, you must be Frank Rio?'

Brad started out of his reverie as a man hailed him from the sidewalk.

Brad reined in as the man walked to the railing. He was a short, thick-set man, clean-shaven and wearing a check shirt and faded Levis. He was toting a gun.

'Like to speak with you, Mr Rio,' the man said. He looked about him furtively as he spoke.

'Go ahead,' Brad replied.

'Not here,' the man continued. 'My place is at Owl Creek, an hour's ride on the trail east outa town. Can you get over there, rightaway?'

'I could if I wasn't heading north,' Brad replied.

The man gripped the rail so hard his knuckles turned white. 'Can't you wait until tomorrow?' he pleaded.

'Maybe it would help if you told me your name and what this is all about,' Brad said.

The man looked around again before replying. 'Name's Jake Griffin. Look, I don't wanna be seen talkin' with you . . . '

As he spoke, a saloon door opened and Tait appeared on the sidewalk, followed by two henchmen.

Brad's attention was distracted for a second and when he looked back, Jake Griffin had disappeared. Tait had spotted Brad and was closing the gap between them rapidly.

'So, we meet again, Mr Rio?' Tait remarked pleasantly. 'Tell me, are you planning on staying in town?'

Brad shook his head. 'Reckon I ain't got no cause to stay,' he replied. 'I'm heading north to see my folks.'

'You're very wise,' Tait said. 'It's never a good idea to get involved with things which don't concern you.'

'Best leave it to the law,' Brad agreed. 'I guess I'm outa touch. By the way,' he said casually, 'who's your boss these days, is it still Major Jones?'

'I believe so,' came the reply.

'Well, I'll be ridin' along,' Brad said. 'Hope you find out who killed the Warrenders.'

'We'll do our best,' Tait replied.

Brad gave Blaze his head and left Paradise at a canter.

When he had departed, Tait said, 'I reckon he knows we ain't Rangers.'

'How come?' asked Dooley.

'Why else would he ask who our boss is?'

'So what do we do now?'

Tait stared at him. 'Jesus! With four thousand dollars at stake, do I have to spell it out?'

6

Brad left Paradise, relieved to shake the dust of the town off his boots. One thing was certain, he wasn't heading north; not after Tait's answer to his perfectly straightforward question about Major Jones. Every Ranger in the service would know that Major Jones, the man in charge of the Frontier Battalion, had died last year. This turned Lisa's testimony into certainty, not that he had ever doubted the girl's word. As one who had spent his life honing skills to enable him to survive, he had an unquestionable faith in the girl's capacity to utilize her remaining four senses to their fullest capacities.

A brief enquiry on the outskirts of town set him on the right trail for Owl Creek. Jake Griffin's invitation intrigued him and his obvious reluctance to be seen by Tait was significant, he was sure of that.

The trail wound across open country punctuated with rocky outcrops that occasionally obscured the view. Although he appeared to be deep in thought, Brad was nevertheless fully aware of the opportunities such terrain offered for surveillance and ambush.

With this in mind, he was not surprised when he saw the glint of a rifle barrel on the summit of an outcrop a couple of hundred yards ahead. At the same time he became aware that he was being followed. He reined in beside an outcrop. With possible danger ahead and behind, it was time to act. He led Blaze off the trail and made him lie down in a shallow gully out of sight of the hidden rifleman. Then he crawled back to the edge of the trail and concealed himself amongst some rocks with such skill that Tait and his men failed to see him as they rode past, although he was only a few yards away from them.

They halted a few yards further on

where the trail opened out giving a view of up to a mile ahead.

'Where the hell is he?' Brad heard one of Tait's men say.

'I always said we should have got on with it,' his companion said.

'Aw shut up the pair of you,' Tait snarled. 'For Christ's sake use your brains. We can't go around killing people in broad daylight, we're supposed to be Rangers. The point is Rio said he was heading north, so why is he headin' east, that's what I want to know?'

'Well we ain't gonna find out, that's fer sure,' Dooley said. 'He's just done disappeared into thin air.'

'Can't have,' Schulze said. 'He must have spotted us and snuck down someplace.'

'Makes sense,' Tait agreed.

'So what do we do? Split up and start lookin'?' Dooley demanded.

'Not unless you want your ass shot off,' Tait said. 'If Rio is a Ranger he could cut all three of us down without battin' an eyelid. In fact it wouldn't surprise me iffen he ain't watchin' us along the barrel of a Winchester right now.'

Schulze suddenly developed the nervous tick in his cheek that always plagued him when he was anxious.

'How does he know we ain't Rangers?' he asked.

'I reckon he suspects it. Why else would he ask who our boss was?'

'So what now?' Dooley demanded.

Tait pondered. 'This trail is heading towards Owl Creek. That's where the biggest bunch of those nesters live.'

'If Rio is a Ranger, maybe he's goin' to speak with them?' Dooley suggested.

Tait nodded. 'I got an idea. Let's go check out this Owl Creek. There's an old saying that Rangers can track like an Indian, shoot like a Kentuckian and fight like the Devil. So keep your eyes skinned.'

Brad waited until Tait and his men had moved away before he stood up.

'Hold it right there, mister!'

He turned to find himself facing a man holding a rifle.

'Now, you best tell me why you're avoiding them Texas Rangers. And it had better be good.'

'Name's Frank Rio,' Brad replied. 'I'm on my way to Owl Creek.'

'So who you got business with?'

'Jake Griffin asked me to meet him there. Unless Tait and his men have been invited to the same meeting, they've chosen to follow me, even though I told him I was headin' north.'

The man tensed. He was slightly built with a weatherbeaten face, calloused hands and nondescript clothes.

'So why should Captain Tait be trailin' you? You on the run or somethin'?'

Brad shook his head. 'I told him I was just passin' through. Maybe he's just checkin' me out.'

'So how come you dodged him? You sure took some findin'. I didn't spot you until you stood up.'

Brad shrugged. 'Tait don't know me.

Maybe he felt he should check me out.'

'Wait a minute, are you the guy who brought in Lisa Warrender after her folks were hung?'

When Brad nodded, the other man extended his hand. 'I'm Sam Parks,' he said. 'I knew Bill and Phoebe Warrender well.' He checked a catch in his throat. 'My wife and me had high hopes that his son would marry my daughter, but now it's not to be, I guess.'

Brad winced. Violent death spread its net of blighted hopes and shattered dreams far wider than people ever imagined.

'I didn't get chance to ask why Jake Griffin wants to see me,' he said.

'Best you hear it from him,' Parks said. 'Owl Creek is twenty minutes' ride from here. It's my turn to keep watch. It's rumoured that Nathan Cowper is sending out a wiring gang. Jake's called a meeting to discuss the situation.'

Brad mounted Blaze and continued his journey. He kept his eyes skinned but he saw nothing of Tait and his men on the way. Owl Creek proved to be a hamlet of several houses clustered round a ford across the creek. A solitary dog yapped at his approach. In a few years Owl Creek could either be a thriving township or it could disappear from the face of the earth.

'Is Jake expectin' you?' A middle-aged woman paused in the act of hanging out her washing and stood, her folded arms supporting a bosom of massive proportions, to cross-examine Brad when he enquired of the where-abouts of Jake Griffin.

'Well in that case you best go round the back of yonder house. All the menfolk are there.'

Brad dismounted and led Blaze in the direction the woman indicated. As he drew closer, he heard the murmur of voices. As he rounded the corner, he was confronted by Jake Griffin and upwards of a dozen men.

'Is this him?' one of the men demanded.

'It's him all right,' Griffin said harshly.

'Let's string up the murderin' bastard!' another man shouted.

Before Brad could take evasive action he was set upon and within moments his Peacemaker was confiscated, his hands tied and a noose placed round his neck. Rough hands propelled him towards the doorway of a barn. Once inside the rope was flung over a roof beam.

'Come on, string him up. What are we waitin' for?' someone shouted.

'Hold it!'

Everyone turned to see the towering bulk of Aaron Tait filling the doorway. His gun was drawn and as he stepped into the darkened barn, Brad saw that his two henchmen were flanking him.

'Enough of this,' Tait said. 'He's my prisoner. You must deliver him into my custody.'

'To stand trial? You must be jokin',' Griffin said. 'I say let's string him up here and now.'

114

'I can't let you do that,' Tait said. He moved towards Brad as he spoke and removed the noose from about his neck. 'I'm a Texas Ranger and it's my job to uphold the law.'

'If this guy murdered the Warrenders and then had the brass neck to bring their daughter into town, he don't deserve no law,' Griffin said.

'That's where you're wrong,' Tait said. 'Texas can't make any progress if it don't abide by the rule of law. It's got to be like that and you know it.'

'So what are you gonna do?' Griffin demanded.

'Take him back to town and arrange for a proper trial.'

'There's no need. We've got twelve men here who'll act as jury.'

'This is a serious crime,' Tait said. 'And then there's the little matter of having a judge present. It's my guess he'll have to be tried in another county to avoid prejudice.'

'This is crazy,' a man protested. 'The further away he gets, the better chance

115

he has of escaping justice.'

Tait shrugged. 'That's the way it is, boys. Now if you'll permit me and my men to go about our duty we'll undertake the job of getting the prisoner back to Paradise.'

Tait sent Dooley to fetch the horses and within minutes they were on their way. The news of Brad's arrest had travelled fast and Brad found himself under the hostile scrutiny of the hamlet's womenfolk as they left.

'So what's this all about?' Brad said when they reached open country. 'I didn't murder the Warrenders.'

Tait grinned. 'They believe it, that's fer sure.' He jerked his thumb over his shoulder in the direction of Owl Creek as he spoke.

'So what now?' Brad demanded.

'Why, now we're clear of Owl Creek, I guess we'll cut you loose.'

'What the hell are you talkin' about?' Dooley demanded.

'Do it. And for Christ's sake quit questioning everything I say.'

Tait drew his pistol and cocked it as Dooley reluctantly began to untie Brad's bonds.

'I get it!' Schulze exulted. 'You're gonna shoot the prisoner while attempting to escape.'

'I reckon that's the first time you've ever figured something out on your own,' Tait said. 'Now hold his horse.'

The sarcasm was lost on Schulze, but Brad wasn't listening. Clearly Tait knew enough about the Rangers to know they once operated the primitive *la ley de fuga*, which allowed them to shoot down any captive trying to make his escape. But not any more — such practice had been abandoned since the days of the late Captain McNelly.

'Before I kill you, Rio, one thing interests me,' Tait said. 'Are you a Texas Ranger?'

'If I am,' Brad replied. 'You're makin' the biggest mistake of your life. As a matter of fact I might ask the same question of you. And I don't believe you are.'

'Ain't a question you're ever gonna see answered, Rio,' Tait said with a laugh.

As the bonds fell away, Brad did the only thing open to him. He gouged his rowels cruelly into Blaze's flanks. It was something he'd never done before in his life. Blaze gave a snort of agony and then shot forward as if all the devils in hell were after him.

Schulze, holding the bridle, never stood a chance. The power of the stallion's forward thrust jerked him clean off his feet and after being dragged a couple of yards he very wisely let go of the bridle rein.

There was a startled shout and then the bullets started to whine. Brad felt a jolt and a sharp stinging pain in his right shoulder. Cursing with pain he held on, spurring Blaze savagely forward along the trail back to Paradise.

The few yards' advantage Brad had gained by surprise gave him all the lead he needed to make good his escape. Weakened as he was by loss of blood from his wound, he realized that if he could make Paradise he stood a chance. Tait might follow him, but he wouldn't cut him down in broad daylight in front of everyone — not until he'd told his lies to the local people.

His surmise was correct. A glance back over his shoulder showed Tait and his men were holding their distance. Tait knew what he was doing; no doubt he figured he could pick Brad up at his leisure once he hit town.

As soon as Brad arrived at the outskirts, he checked Blaze into a steady canter. The wound in his shoulder needed dressing.

What to do?

There was only one place he could go — the Warrenders. He hesitated. To put these good people at risk, especially Lisa, was unforgivable, but where else could he go?

Riding as normally as possible, he left the main street and took a circuitous route to the rear of the Warrenders' house. As he dismounted by the gate, he was relieved to see Lisa sitting in the shade cast by the house on a bench by the open door. A cat was dozing in a patch of sunlight on the grass beside her.

'Who is it?' the girl enquired softly as he tethered Blaze to the garden fence.

'It's me, Frank Rio,' Brad said as he approached her. 'Is your grandmother in?'

At that moment Hester Warrender appeared in the doorway.

'Mr Rio!' she exclaimed. 'What on earth's happened? Your shirt is covered in blood.'

'Are you hurt?' Lisa said, her voice rising in alarm.

Hester ushered him into the house and sat him on a wooden chair in the kitchen. She cut Brad's shirt free with a pair of scissors and inspected the wound.

'I guess you're lucky,' she opined. 'The bullet grazed you. But you'll have to rest to help the bleeding stop.'

Whilst the kettle came to a boil on

the fire, she rummaged in a drawer and emerged with what Brad recognized as an army field-dressing.

'How come you have one of them?' he enquired as she cleaned the wound and applied it expertly.

'I served in the war as a nurse,' Hester replied. She handed Brad one of her husband's shirts to put on. 'I put more of these on at Gettysburg than I care to remember. This is a fleabite compared to the wounds some of them poor boys endured. More to the point, how about telling me how this happened?'

Brad saw little point in not giving her a full account of the day's events.

'So Tait's got the upper hand,' Hester said. 'If all the people at Owl Creek believe he and his men are Rangers, what can you do?'

'Don't forget that I know differently,' Lisa said quietly.

'I don't want it you should be involved,' Brad said vehemently.

'Why? Do you think a jury won't

believe me because I'm blind?' The anger in the girl's voice was palpable.

'I guess that's the way things might be,' Hester said gently. 'Meantime,' she said to Brad, 'what are you gonna do?'

'One thing's certain — I can't stay here,' he replied. 'Tait and his men are gonna come lookin' for me. I can't put you good people at risk.'

'Where are you going to go?' Hester demanded. 'You aren't fit to travel for a day or two, that's for sure.'

'Ssh! — someone is coming up the path,' Lisa warned.

Brad's right hand shot for the empty holster by his side as he heard the knock on the front door.

'I'll go,' Hester said.

Lisa clung to Brad's arm in terror as they heard her grandmother open the door.

'Why, good afternoon, ma'am.' Tait's voice carried clearly through the house. 'We're lookin' for Frank Rio. He escaped from custody earlier today.'

'He escaped from custody? What do

you mean?' Hester demanded.

'Seems like you and your granddaughter had a lucky escape,' Tait told her. 'He is the one who murdered your folks. His befriendin' the girl was mighty smart cover. Almost had me fooled. Has he passed this way by any chance?'

'No, he hasn't,' Hester said tartly. 'But if he does I'll know what to do.'

'That's the spirit, ma'am. The sooner we get this murderin', low-down skunk to the gallows the better. Good day to you.'

Hester closed the door and returned to the kitchen.

'My, I've never told such lies. May God forgive me,' she said in some agitation.

'Isn't Mr Rio's horse still tethered outside?' asked Lisa.

Brad rose to his feet. 'Not for much longer,' he said. 'I'm pullin' out.'

'You shouldn't ride until that wound has closed,' Hester said.

'I just need someplace to lie up for a coupla days,' Brad said. 'One thing is certain, I can't stay here.'

'Where will you go?' Lisa asked anxiously.

'Where my fancy takes me, I guess.'

Hester walked over to a drawer and took out an old Army Colt and an ammo-pouch.

'Best you take this,' she said. 'Belongs to Jacob, I know it works because he takes it out and fires it every now and then but I guess he's no use for such things any more.'

'I'm obliged to you, ma'am,' Brad said, as he loaded the weapon.

'Don't worry, child, he's one of life's survivors,' Hester said as she watched Brad's departure.

'I wish I could be so sure,' Lisa said.

Her grandmother looked at her fondly.

Why, I do believe my precious little lamb has taken a shine to him!

The words had scarcely formed inside her head when a shot rang out followed by another . . .

7

Tait returned to his men who were waiting in the road outside the Warrenders' house.

'He's in there,' he said curtly. 'There's blood on the old woman's apron.'

'So what are we waiting for? Let's go in and get him.'

Tait took out the makings and rolled a smoke.

'One of these days you guys will learn to use your brains,' he said. He lit the cigarette and exhaled a lungful of smoke. 'If Rio is in there, he knows I've stopped by. He ain't gonna want to put those females at risk so he'll leave pronto.'

'So what do we do, boss?' Schulze asked.

'Ned, you and me will cover both ends of the back road; Pete, you cover the front. And keep outa sight, the pair of you.'

'What do we do if we see him?'

'It's common knowledge he's a wanted man now. Gun the bastard down.'

★　★　★

In the private room at the Cattlemen's Club, Judge Banyon looked appreciatively at a glass of whiskey before he downed it.

'Well?' asked Cowper.

Fife drew easily on his pipe; he was a man of few words.

'Everything is fine,' Banyon said. 'Captain Tait and his men have discovered who was responsible for the murder of the Warrender family. He and his men are apprehending him as we speak.'

'So who was it?' Cowper asked heavily.

'A guy called Frank Rio. He told Sheriff Rance he was just passing through. He had the effrontery to bring the Warrender girl into town.'

'She's blind, isn't she?' Fife enquired.

Banyon nodded. 'How low can you get? I don't know the whys and the wherefores, but he must have figured there's no way a jury will accept her evidence when she couldn't see anything.'

Fife cleared his throat. 'One thing puzzles me. *Why* did Rio bring the girl in, I wonder?'

Banyon poured himself another whiskey. 'Who knows how such a man's mind works? He might live a perfectly normal life and then suddenly his brain turns a cartwheel. I once met an outlaw who posed as a Texas Ranger. He got away literally with murder because no one ever questioned his credentials.'

'But to escort the Lister girl back to her grandparents — I find that bizarre,' Fife continued.

'As I said,' Banyon replied, 'there's no accounting for it. But one thing is certain; he's done us a big favour inasmuch as the fence-cutters are now leaderless. Joe Lister is injured and I don't think the rest have the spunk to resist.' He raised his glass. 'I'll give you a toast, gentlemen — to a bright future . . . without let or hindrance to our plans.'

★ ★ ★

Brad emerged from the back of the house and walked down the path. As he untethered Blaze, his eyes were everywhere, assessing hiding-places for a possible ambush. The access at the back was a narrow lane flanked with the wicket fences of the houses on either side.

He was just about to get into the saddle when he saw a bush twitch just beyond him to the right. He paused. The movement had come near a wooden shed that he surmised was the rear of a livery barn. Glancing over his shoulder he saw another movement, this time near the wheel of a parked buggy.

'We got you covered, Rio, there's no escape this time. Best you surrender right now.'

Brad recognized Tait's voice.

For answer he let go of Blaze's bridle, slapped his rear with his hat and as the stallion trotted forward riderless, he vaulted the fence into the next garden further on from the Warrenders'. The movement attracted the curiosity of the man ahead and as he peered round the corner of the livery barn, Brad loosed off a snap shot which was accurate enough to make his adversary withdraw hurriedly. As soon as Brad had fired he made a dive to the left.

Tait spotted Brad's first move, but was unprepared for the next and he riddled the original spot with a hail of bullets. Brad responded with another shot accurate enough to force Tait to keep his head down. Brad peered ahead. Blaze had reached the end of the road and had stopped as if to await further instructions.

'It's no good, Rio. Like I said, you're trapped. Surrender now while you still got a chance,' Tait shouted.

For answer, Brad vaulted the fence into the next garden. He was getting close to Tait's man now. The guy was getting jumpy for he loosed off a couple of shots that went nowhere near Brad.

'Save it, Ned,' Tait shouted. 'Don't let him draw your fire.'

Brad winced. That was a soldier talking. He had to take care himself, for the percussion Army Colt was not as quick to reload as the modern Peace-maker.

Brad pondered for a few seconds. If he could enter the next garden along it would bring him level with the guy hiding behind the livery barn. Tait would be expecting him to vault the fence, but the range was too long for an accurate shot. The guy opposite was the greater threat.

Brad crawled on his hands and knees across the garden until he came to the corner of the garden. The silence was unnerving. Were his opponents changing position or were they just waiting for him to make a mistake?

Still on his hands and knees, he peered through the gaps in the rails. The guy opposite was still there, only ten yards away across the road. He could just see part of his hat protruding beyond the end of the building. He screwed his neck round and stared intently the other way but could see no sign of Tait. That meant nothing — he could have crawled forward to a new position without Brad seeing him. Indeed, Brad must assume that he had done so.

'Where the hell is he?' the guy behind the livery barn shouted.

The tone of his voice suggested to Brad he was edgy.

'You stay put, Ned. We got him trapped. He ain't goin' anywhere.'

Tait's voice was much closer. Brad figured he was approaching along the opposite side of the lane, following the garden fences, much as he himself had done.

'Hold your fire!' Tait shouted urgently. 'Someone's comin'.'

Brad stared in disbelief when he saw Lisa approaching along the road, tapping a walking stick gently along the fence as she did so.

'Lisa, go back, please,' he implored as she drew level with the garden in which he was hiding.

'Oh Mr Rio,' she said. 'I am going to visit my grandfather at the store. Perhaps you would kindly escort me there?'

She spoke clearly and confidently. Plainly she intended Tait and his men to hear every word.

Brad hesitated.

'Please, Mr Rio,' Lisa said. 'I need to learn my way about town. I can't stay indoors all the time.'

Brad rose to his feet, holstered his weapon, and hopped over the fence into the lane.

'Thank you, Mr Rio, you are very

kind.' Lisa slipped her arm inside his as she spoke.

Tait said nothing as the couple walked to the end of the lane. The only sound was the eerie tap-tap of the girl's stick against the wicket fencing. When they reached the end of the lane, Blaze appeared with a soft whicker.

'That was a crazy thing to do, Lisa,' Brad muttered as, leading the stallion with one hand and holding the girl with the other, they made their way towards her grandfather's store.

'I believe it has saved your life, and that's all that matters,' Lisa replied. 'Not even scum like Tait would dare shoot me in broad daylight.'

'I am truly grateful,' Brad replied. 'But don't ever pull a stunt like this again,' he said as they reached the steps to the boardwalk.

'Is Tait still following us?' Lisa enquired.

Brad glanced over his shoulder. 'Yes, but he's keeping his distance.'

When they reached the boardwalk,

Brad said, 'The door to the shop is in front of you now.'

'I believe you must leave town now,' Lisa said. 'Get on that beautiful horse and ride like the wind.'

'But . . . '

'Just go.'

To Brad's infinite astonishment she leaned up and kissed him on the cheek.

'Take care,' she whispered. 'Now go.'

He left the girl, went down the steps and as he mounted Blaze he saw Tait and one of his men still standing at the end of the lane, watching him intently. Brad raised his hat in a mock salute and set Blaze into a swinging canter, heading out of town.

★　★　★

'I heard firing. What happened?' Schulze asked Tait when they met up a few minutes later.

'Nothing,' came the reply.

'How come? You were two against one.'

'Because the guy is as crafty as they come. That blind girl appeared and he used her as cover to get away.'

'Do you reckon she planned on helping him?' Dooley asked.

'I'm certain of it,' Tait replied. 'Pity we didn't hang her with the rest.'

'Maybe we'll deal with her later,' Schulze said. He uttered a sneering laugh. 'Pity she can't see what I'm gonna do to her.'

'So what'll we do now?' Schulze asked.

'We'll go see the sheriff and organize a posse.'

'So we're still posin' as Rangers?'

'No reason for us not to. I figure Rio's wound might just hold him back. So let's go get after him.'

* * *

Once clear of the town, Brad became conscious that his wound was paining him. The exertion must have opened it and his shoulder felt sore and so stiff he

135

could hardly move his arm.

Like Hester Warrender said, he was in need of a couple of days' rest to get his wound closed. Where could he go? His first thought was the Listers' place, but he dismissed it instantly. Tait would be organizing a pursuit, perhaps even a posse, and he dared not put the family at risk. Tait must have figured he was at the Warrenders' before he set up the ambush. Would there be any consequences for Lisa and her grandmother? He thought not. Tait would be too busy trumping up charges against him to be concerned about them.

There was only one place he could hole up — Sandy Creek.

Having made up his mind he expended what little energy he had left in covering his trail. This took time, but when he had finished he was convinced that only an experienced Indian tracker would know where to find him.

It was dusk when he crossed the creek and reached the soddy. A sombre atmosphere hung over the deserted dwelling but he was too tired to be influenced by it. He stabled Blaze and after consuming a can of beans and a mug of coffee, dog-tired, he was preparing to bed down for the night when he heard the sound of an approaching rider . . .

★　★　★

Tait lost no time in organizing a pursuit. Touring the town with Sheriff Rance, he explained the reason for his need for a posse to the citizens who saw no reason to disbelieve his claim to be a Ranger. And this made Frank Rio's behaviour even more reprehensible.

When one man enquired as to why the fugitive had gone back to the Warrenders, Tait replied:

'Now you see the measure of a man who can dupe a blind girl and an old woman. He even used the girl as cover to make his escape. Believe me, gentlemen, your women and children are not safe while this man is still loose. We must find him and bring him to justice as soon as possible.'

Tait's testimony was so firmly believed that within an hour he had assembled a posse of some twenty men. Rance did not conceal his relief when Tait ordered him to remain in Paradise 'lest this monster should make an unwelcome return'.

From enquiries made *en route*, Tait established that his quarry had left town on the route due south. However, as the posse proceeded, doubts began to be expressed as to whether they were on the right trail. When they came to the place where Banyon had fenced off the trail, many of the riders expressed their discontent. The situation was compounded by the fact that no one was carrying wirecutters and they were forced to tie ropes around the fence poles and snap them off before a way through could be made. This cost a great deal of time and effort and an aura of bad temper hung over the posse as it resumed the pursuit. Tait kept his counsel, but made a mental note that there was very little sympathy for Banyon.

'If he came this way, he surely must have passed Joe Lister's place,' a grizzled old-timer remarked.

'Right,' Tait agreed.

★ ★ ★

Charlie was fetching a pail of water up from the creek when the thunder of horses' hoofs attracted her attention. She put down her bucket and ran up to the house, but her mother had heard it too and the two women waited in silence as the posse splashed through the creek and came to a halt in front of them.

'I'm Captain Tait of the Rangers,' Tait announced. He removed his hat and flashed a dazzling smile at Charlie. 'Why, I believe we have already met?'

Charlie did not return his overture. She maintained a tight-lipped silence.

'We're seekin' a guy name of Frank Rio who we believe has passed this way,' Tait continued.

'Frank Rio? Why, he was here the other day, but we haven't seen him since,' Mrs Lister said. 'Mind tellin' me what's goin' on?'

'He's wanted for the murder of the Warrender family.'

'That can't be true!' Charlie cried. 'Why, he helped me and Lisa. He took her to her grandparents and brought me home.'

'Shows you what a cunning desperado he is, ma'am,' Tait replied. 'Who would have thought a man could commit murder and then behave like that? He has already escaped custody. We believe he's wounded so he may be seeking help. Believe me, ladies, we are dealing here with a very dangerous criminal indeed.'

'Well, he hasn't stopped by here since we last saw him,' Mrs Lister said.

'Bearing in mind he's a slippery customer, mind if we check your place out?'

Mrs Lister shrugged. 'Help yourself. We got nothing to hide.'

The two women waited in silence as the posse men with guns drawn, searched every square inch of the farmstead.

'Nary a sign of him,' Schulze reported when they had finished.

'I guess we need a tracker,' a posse man said.

'Major Banyon has an Indian on his payroll,' another said. 'A Comanche called Little Eagle.'

'Why don't we go fetch him?' Schulze suggested.

'OK. We'll do that,' Tait agreed.

When the posse had left, Mrs Lister rounded on Charlie.

'You sure you haven't seen Frank Rio today?' Charlie shook her head. 'There's somethin' bad goin' on here, Ma. I can't believe he's a murderer, can you?'

Her mother shook her head.

'He must have come this way,' she said. 'So where has he got to?'

Charlie clicked her fingers. 'I bet he's turned off the trail and holed up at the Warrenders' place.'

Mrs Lister shrugged. 'Could be.'

'It he's wounded, he may need help,' Charlie persisted. 'I'm gonna saddle up and ride over to Sandy Creek while it's still light.'

'You'll do no such thing,' her mother said.

'Don't try to stop me, Ma,' Charlie replied. 'I'm twenty-one, not twelve.'

Taken aback by her daughter's tone, Mrs Lister stared at her.

'What's your father going to say?'

'Nothing if you don't tell him. Anyway I don't care if you do, my mind is made up.'

Charlie went to the barn and reappeared leading her sorrel, already saddled and bridled.

'What if Captain Tait is right and this man Rio is a murderer?' her mother demanded.

Charlie smiled. 'Ma, I know you think I'm still wet behind the ears, but I know, I just know that that man Tait is either wrong or just plain lying.'

'Why should a Texas Ranger lie?' her mother said as Charlie sprang into the saddle.

'That's what I'm gonna find out,' said Charlie.

8

Jesus! Has Tait found me already, Brad thought as he reached for his gun.

He rose to his feet and moved cautiously towards the door. There was only one rider, which puzzled him. It was almost dark, but not quite, which added to his discomfiture. The wound in his shoulder stung abominably and for the first time in his life he felt old as well as tired.

Peering through the door, gun at the ready, he caught sight of the approaching rider coming through the creek. Little silver droplets cascaded, winking like jewels in the fading light.

The rider left the creek and started purposefully towards the house. Brad opened the door and stepped outside.

'Hold it right there!'

His command rang out so loud, the rider's horse shied. Brad waited whilst the rider regained control. 'Frank, it's me.'

He lowered his gun and stepped forward.

'Why, Charlie!' he exclaimed. 'What the hell are you doin' here?'

'That guy Tait and a posse stopped by at our place. They said they were lookin' for you, Frank, and they mean business.' She led her horse forward on the bridle. 'Tait said it was you who killed the Warrenders. Tell me it's not true, Frank, please!'

Brad stared at her.

'D'you really believe that, Charlie?'

To his astonishment the tough frontier girl burst into tears.

'If I really believed Tait,' she said between sobs, 'would I have come out here to find you at this time of night?'

Brad took the horse from her. He put his good arm round her shoulders as they walked to the barn.

They stabled her horse and when they returned Brad set about making coffee.

'Tait said you were wounded,' Charlie said as she recovered her composure.

'It ain't nuthin',' Brad replied. 'Just a scratch.'

'Let me look.' The girl picked up a candle as she spoke. She gave a sharp intake of breath. 'Jesus! Your shirt's covered with blood. Take it off. How did you get this?' Charlie set about removing the blood-soaked dressing.

She listened in silence as Brad gave her a brief account of his pursuit and denunciation by Tait, his subsequent escape and ambush.

'That was very brave of Lisa. You seem to have gone looking for trouble,' Charlie remarked.

He winced as she completed the task of cleaning the wound.

'What I don't understand,' she continued, 'is why Tait should want to pin something on you that you didn't do.'

Brad pondered whilst she commenced to tear up some bed-linen for a bandage.

'Well?' she asked. 'You haven't answered my question.'

'Because Tait is not what he says he is,' he replied.

Charlie listened, wide-eyed in the candlelight, whilst he told her the full story. He concluded by showing her the badge that proclaimed his office, tucked away in his lower vest-pocket.

'But if you are a Ranger, how come you didn't say so right at the beginning? Why do you skulk around not wearin' your badge?'

'With hindsight, you have a point,' Brad conceded. 'But I often choose to go about incognito, it can be useful sometimes. I guess I was caught on the wrong foot over that business with the wire across the road. When Tait turned up I had a suspicion then that he wasn't a Ranger, but I've never served in this part of Texas before and I wasn't convinced until Lisa told me she recognized his voice as one of her family's murderers.'

Charlie shivered. 'Poor Lisa, I can't

believe her folks are buried outside.'

'Of one thing I'm certain,' Brad said. 'If I'd revealed who I was to Collier and his men, I believe Tait would have shot me before you arrived.'

'And claimed *you* were an impostor?' Brad nodded.

'And now it's too late,' Charlie said. 'By now, Tait will have gotten the whole town believing you are a murderer.'

'Somebody has got to be behind this,' Brad mused. 'My guess is it's Banyon.'

'You oughta get some rest,' Charlie said. 'You're tuckered out.'

'What about you?' Brad said. 'You gotta get back home.'

Charlie shook her head. 'No I ain't. I'm stayin' right here with you.'

★ ★ ★

'We lost his trail,' Tait told Banyon. 'I've sent the posse home. What I need is to borrow your Indian and we'll soon find him.'

'I don't believe I'm hearing this,'

Banyon said. He got up from behind his desk and began to pace his office. 'You're seriously telling me that he gave three of you the slip not once, not twice, but three times?'

'If Dooley had done as he was told, this would never have happened,' Tait growled.

Banyon almost smiled. He was enjoying Tait's discomfiture.

'That's just why you never made it beyond lieutenant,' he said. 'A good officer never blames his men. How will you proceed?'

'First light we'll get Little Eagle on to tracking him. We'll not bother with a posse — a dozen of your boys will do. He won't escape this time, I promise you.'

★ ★ ★

Brad awoke with a start. Familiar with the night sounds of the wilderness, even while dormant his senses responded to the slightest unfamiliarity. The hoot of

149

an owl, the scrabble of armadillo going about their nocturnal business were both, in the relevant parts of Texas, sounds so deeply embedded in his sensory perceptions as not to disturb his slumber.

But this — *this* — was different. It was a man-made sound. The sound of something wriggling along the ground like a snake.

Only it wasn't a snake . . .

Brad lay for a few moments, knowing the value of patience in such situations. To rush outside blindly was to court disaster. The night air was warm. On retirement, Charlie had bunked down, a couple of yards away from him, fully clothed on the floor of the cabin without demur. He listened intently, filtering out the rhythmic sound of the girl's breathing.

Had he been dreaming? He wished he had. Bitter experience had taught him to trust his own judgement and that peculiar sixth sense which had retrieved so many situations in the past.

150

There it was again! Closer this time. To his finely tuned ear it was the unmistakable sound of the stealthy approach. Whoever it was lurking out there, he knew his business, for he was planning his approach at random intervals, sometimes leaving as much as five minutes between moves. To Brad that meant only one thing — the man creeping up towards the house must be an Indian.

How far away was he now?

Gathering his faculties, Brad picked up his gun and rose to his feet. On feet as light as a cat's paws he crept towards the door. It hung slightly ajar on its leather hinges. He lowered himself slowly into a squatting position and peered through the opening.

A full moon illuminated the landscape with a blue light, casting deep shadows from the rocky outcrops, reflected in the bed of the creek as a gleaming crescent. In any other situation Brad would have been content to observe the scene, to draw an inner strength from its sublimeness, but now its iridescent beauty seemed evil and threatening. Had Tait and his men lingered on such a night before they perpetrated their atrocity on the Warrender family? In his mind's eye he could see the corpses swinging gently in the breeze. Once again the hand of man had ravaged the wilderness, taken away its innocence and wrought savagery where all was at peace and harmony.

When he was a boy, Brad had been the first to find his father's body on the range with an arrow embedded in his back. The experience was etched in his mind with a peculiar intensity and since then, during his passage through life, he had made it his business to acquire knowledge concerning the ways of the Indian.

And so he resisted the temptation to open the door wider. The Indian would be watching, waiting for the slightest movement that would betray his presence. And he could not afford to make a mistake, for he was mindful of his responsibility towards the girl, who was still sleeping peacefully behind him.

Holding his gun in readiness, he waited until he heard the faint rustle that betrayed another approach. Only someone completely in tune with the wilderness would detect it. By now he was certain that there was only one man out there. If anyone was approaching the rear of the cabin he was confident that Blaze's soft whicker would tell him so. In any event, the days of the mass Indian attack on an isolated settler's dwelling were now long gone.

By now he had placed the unwelcome visitor as being some thirty yards away and slightly to the left, just out of direct sight of the open door.

What to do? If Brad opened the door, he would frame himself in the moonlight, making himself a perfect target. All he could do was wait and see how close the man would come.

But his adversary was smarter than that. All was quiet for a few moments and then, suddenly, a pebble landed on the ground in front of the door.

In the stillness of the night, the noise sounded shockingly loud. Only Brad's iron self-discipline prevented him from reacting. He glanced back at the girl. To his relief, she was still asleep.

You ain't gonna catch me out as easy as that, he thought.

He removed a shell from his gunbelt and, leaning forward, with a flick of his wrist he threw it through the opening.

As it landed he heard a slight guttural grunt. Brad waited, listening intently before trying another look through the door. His keen eyes caught a fleeting, wraith-like movement in terrain leading down to the creek. He opened the door a little wider to confirm his belief. Yes, he was right, the shadowy figure of a man was retreating towards the creek.

Brad gave a wry smile as he drew back into the cabin. In the battle of wits, his opponent had emerged the winner for there was no doubt in his mind that Tait had sent a scout to ascertain if he were here. It was the only possible explanation.

'What's the matter?'

The girl's voice startled him out of his thoughts. She was staring at him, wide-eyed and suddenly he realized he must have aroused her fear because he was still holding his gun.

'It's OK,' he told her as he slipped the weapon back into its holster. 'I guess I couldn't sleep. I got to hearin' things, so I got up and had me a look around. Sorry if I disturbed you.'

Charlie rose to her feet. 'Do you think Tait will find us here?' she asked him.

With an effort, Brad restrained his urge to make a rapid departure, for he didn't want to alarm her.

'If we stay, then I guess maybe he will.'

She stood before him, looking strangely vulnerable in the moonlit room. To resist the urge to take her into his arms and kiss her would have made him less than a man.

'Oh, Brad,' she whispered as they

broke apart. 'I'm frightened.'

He stroked her hair gently. In contrast to her bravado when she had confronted Tait and his men at the wire, she seemed now little more than a terrified girl.

'We gotta get outa here,' he said. 'Dawn's breaking and I figure it could only be a matter of time before Tait shows up.'

'How's the shoulder?' Charlie enquired.

'A bit stiff, but it'll be OK, I guess,' Brad replied.

He held his spyglass to one eye and carefully traversed the countryside as he spoke.

'So where will we go?' Charlie asked.

'You ain't gonna like this,' Brad said, 'but I'd like it for you to saddle up right now and head back home.'

Charlie laid her hand on his arm. 'Why don't we leave this place together? We could go anywhere we want and Tait will never find us.'

Brad rounded on her. 'Why, Charlie, what are you thinkin' of? You shouldn't be here with me right now. Good women don't carry on this way.'

'You sound just like my parents!' she flashed back.

'Maybe that's the way it should sound,' Brad retorted. 'But that apart, you're forgettin' that I'm here to bring law and order to this county. I can't just ride off when it suits me.'

Charlie looked crestfallen. 'I'm sorry,' she said.

'You need to leave right now,' Brad said. He snapped the spyglass shut and pocketed it as he spoke. 'There's a group of riders heading this way. Best you saddle up and leave the back way. I take it you know the country well enough to circle your way back home?'

Charlie nodded. Together they walked round the back of the house to the stable.

'What are you gonna do?' she asked anxiously as she tightened the cinch on her saddle.

'I'll cover your tracks and draw 'em off in the opposite direction,' he replied as he did the same. 'Now go.'

She hesitated.

'Go on!' Brad urged. 'Don't worry about me. I can take care of myself, I promise you.'

To emphasize his words, he took off his hat and slapped the backside of her sorrel.

Charlie spurred the animal forward for a few yards before reining him in again. Brad eased Blaze forward until they were level.

She gazed at him with frank blue eyes that told him what she was about to say.

'I love you, Brad,' she said.

He stared at her. Why should he feel so surprised at something he'd been vaguely aware of since they had first met? Maybe he had shut it out of his mind. He had met women aplenty who had toyed with his emotions but this young girl's frank admission, wrung out in such desperate circumstances, rocked him to the core.

'Please take care of yourself, Brad,' she pleaded. 'I couldn't bear it if anything should happen to you.'

Behind him Brad heard faint sounds of the approaching riders.

'For God's sake, go, Charlie,' he muttered, 'while you still have time.'

Brad watched her leave, knowing that the first part of his plan was now under way. Tait would certainly put his tracker's skills to use and when he arrived it wouldn't be long before he discovered that two people had spent the night at the soddy. By sending Charlie off in a different direction he hoped to confuse the issue even further, for the tracker would not be able to differentiate between her horse and his at this stage. His plan was simple in conception but required skill to implement. It hinged on his ability to cover Charlie's trail so that she could not be followed. Tait and his men would therefore be drawn on to himself and Charlie's identity would be kept secret. That done, all he had to do was deal with Tait and his henchmen.

He smiled grimly. If only it were that simple . . .

★ ★ ★

'OK, boys,' Tait said to his men as they reached the creek. 'We know he's in there. He's as slippery as an eel, so keep your eyes skinned and don't let him get away this time. Ned, take three men and cover the place from the right. Pete, take another three and head left and then we got him surrounded.'

Little Eagle stirred uneasily. He hadn't told Tait of the ploy he'd used to discover whether the house was occupied. He was an elderly man now, and given the reputation of the man they were pursuing, he hadn't felt disposed to take undue risk. And he had been proved right. The response to his throwing the pebble had been so immediate it had surprised him. Instinctively he knew he was up against a man who was his equal in all the skills it had taken him a lifetime to

160

acquire. The man must have been aware of his approach for far longer than ever he could have imagined, maybe even had him in the sights of a rifle . . .

'Let's check the place out,' Tait said. 'Let one man hold the horses, the rest dismount, spread out and approach the house using available cover.'

For the next ten minutes, the ten men forming Tait's group crawled on their bellies along the ground in a painfully slow approach towards the house.

'I thought you said he was in there,' Tait snapped at Little Eagle.

'He was,' the Indian replied. 'But maybe he has gone now.'

Tait nodded. By now he was so close to the house he was convinced it wasn't occupied.

A few yards from the house he stood up and walked inside.

'The place is deserted,' he told his companions as they joined him. He rounded on Little Eagle. 'You sure he was here last night? Let's hope either Pete or Ned have spotted him.'

Little Eagle picked up two plates.

'I think two people spend night here,' he said.

'So how do you know one of them was Frank Rio?' Tait demanded.

'I said that there was someone in the house,' Little Eagle replied. 'I did not say who it was or how many.'

They walked round the back.

'Sign here,' Little Eagle said. 'It show two horses leave at sunrise.'

'Let's hope for your sake that Pete or Ned have spotted them,' Tait growled.

* * *

Dooley and Schulze dispersed with their complement of Banyon's men as instructed.

A few minutes later, to Schulze's delight, as he and his men waited in concealment beside a rock, he saw Charlie approaching them.

'Well, now, Miss Lister,' he drawled.

'I wonder what brings you this way at the crack of dawn?'

Charlie started as the four men emerged from the shadow of the rock.

'What business is it of yours?' she shot back.

'Miss, I guess you're forgettin' that I'm a Texas Ranger investigatin' the murder of the Warrender family. And when someone appears from the direction of their house at this hour of the day, I get to wonderin' what they've been up to.'

Charlie stared at her interrogator and his companions, men she recognized as Banyon's hands. Did they really believe Tait and his men were what they claimed to be? It was on the tip of her tongue to denounce this grinning jackanapes out of hand, but Banyon's men wouldn't believe her, that was certain.

'Well, miss, seein' as you won't answer, might I suggest you come along with us and see my boss.'

To Charlie's horror, the four men

surrounded her and escorted her in the direction of the Warrenders' house.

As they approached, she was aware of a large body of men and horses close to the house. Tait was among them.

'Where the hell did you find *her*?' he snapped as Schulze drew up.

'She was heading away from here,' Schulze said. 'I reckon she's spent the night in the house.'

Tait hooked his thumbs in his gunbelt.

'With whom?' he said with an evil smile.

'That's none of your business,' she replied.

'Well, now, Miss Lister, I guess you've caused us trouble enough already. My guess is that you were with Frank Rio. Maybe you can tell me where he is headin' for?'

'Why should I know where Frank Rio is?' Charlie said defiantly. 'I ain't his keeper.'

'Don't try my patience,' Tait snapped. 'I know you spent the night here with him. I suppose he's lookin' after his own skin as usual. I guess your pa is gonna be mighty pleased when he finds out what his daughter's been up to.'

When Charlie didn't reply, he said, 'Well, I guess your failure to inform us of Rio's whereabouts could be taken as obstructing the course of justice.'

'Want me to take her into town?' Schulze asked.

Tait shook his head. 'Take her back home. Maybe her parents will make her see sense,' he declared. 'It don't need four of you to escort a woman home,' he pointed out as Schulze made to leave. 'Just take one with you. He can go back and report to his boss when you've done.'

'What'll I do then?' Schulze asked.

'Go back into town and inform the citizens we're on a hunt for Rio.' Tait turned to Little Eagle. 'Now's your chance to do your job properly. Find me Rio's trail and let's go get him this time.'

9

It was late afternoon when Jake Griffin rode into Paradise. He reined in outside Jacob Warrender's store, dismounted and after tethering his sorrel he went inside.

There he found the old-timer and his wife, Hester, with their granddaughter.

'Howdy, folks,' Griffin said, removing his hat. 'I guess you'll have heard the news by now? It looks like your granddaughter has had a lucky escape.'

Jacob looked puzzled. 'How come you make that out?'

Griffin smiled. 'Ain't you heard? Captain Tait and his men have arrested Frank Rio. I guess he'll be coolin' his heels in jail right now.'

'It's you who's behind, Jake,' Hester said quietly. She looked across at her husband, who was busy tamping his pipe with tobacco. 'Don't you think it's high time this town knew the truth, Jacob?'

'We already know the truth,' Griffin said. 'That Frank Rio's one of the slipperiest outlaws I've ever heard of.' He glanced at Lisa. 'To think how he deceived your granddaughter! How low can a man stoop, I wonder?'

'I believe you are Mr Griffin, from Owl Creek?' Lisa said quietly.

'Why that's so,' he replied. 'Why, I'm real sorry I didn't introduce myself, Miss Lisa. That was very remiss of me, I guess.'

'That's quite all right, Mr Griffin,' Lisa replied. 'I never forget a voice. And I tell you, I'll never forget the voices of of the men who killed my family.'

Griffin twiddled his hat nervously.

'I'm real sorry about it, Miss Lisa, we all are. We'll all be glad when this miscreant is brought to justice. Hangin' is too good for the likes of men like Frank Rio.'

'It wasn't Frank Rio who murdered my family,' Lisa said quietly. 'It was the man who calls himself Captain Tait and his men who did it.'

Jake Griffin stared at her.

'Why, Miss Lisa, that can't be right, Captain Tait and his men are Texas Rangers.'

Lisa shook her head. 'Tait and his men are impostors,' she told him. 'Frank Rio is a Ranger, only that isn't his real name.'

'Well, now, Miss Lisa,' Griffin said with a splutter. 'With all due respect for your condition, how can you be sure of what you say?'

'I am as sure of it as of anything I have been in my life,' Lisa replied quietly.

'Recollect she knew who you were without asking,' Hester pointed out.

'I still don't believe it!' Griffin exclaimed.

'You best had,' Jacob Warrender said. Clouds of smoke almost hid his face as he lit his pipe. 'What better cover could the cattlemen have used to get rid of your leader than to bring in an outlaw masquerading as a Texas Ranger?'

There was a pause as the slow dawn of understanding illuminated Jake Griffin's features.

'You sayin' that Banyon and his cronies have fixed this?' Griffin demanded.

'Figure it out,' Jacob replied. 'And when you're through you'd best round up your friends and get after Tait before he does anyone else any harm.'

★ ★ ★

'I take it you know the way?' Schulze enquired of his companion as they set forth. He had taken the precaution of attaching a rope with which he could lead Charlie's horse.

The man gave a surly nod. He made little secret of the fact that he didn't relish the idea of being relegated to escort duty. In fact he was privately dreading the ribbing he would get from the hands when they found out, for there had been some quarrelling over which of them should be released from duty to accompany the Texas Rangers.

The journey continued in silence, but the way Schulze kept glancing back at her with a knowing smile made Charlie feel uneasy. The fellow was plotting something, she was sure.

And so it happened that when they reached the trail from Paradise, Schulze said to his companion:

'OK, I reckon I know the way from here. Best you go report to Judge Banyon like the boss said, hey?'

The man needed no further encouragement. Schulze gave a chuckle as he watched him leave.

'OK, that just leaves you and me,' he said to Charlie.

Charlie froze as his lascivious eyes swept over her.

'Pretty, ain't you? Why I swear you're the prettiest gal I set eyes on since I hit Paradise.'

When Charlie didn't reply, he spurred his horse gently forward, drawing her after him. After a mile or so, they came to a stream, a tributary of the one that ran past her house. 'Guess the horses need a drink,' Schulze said.

Charlie dismounted reluctantly. Together they led the animals forward to a suitable place on the bank.

'So what are you gonna tell your daddy 'bout where you spent the night then?' Schulze enquired.

Charlie did not like the way he smirked as he spoke.

'It's none of your business,' she said stubbornly.

'Ah, but it is,' Schulze said. 'You're forgettin' I am a Texas Ranger.'

Charlie took a deep breath, but before she could speak again he said:

'I wonder what your daddy will say when he finds out you spent the night with a wanted man?'

'But . . . '

'Now you just hear me out,' Schulze went on. He had drawn so close she could smell the rank odour of his breath on the still morning air. ''Cos there ain't no need for him to find out a thing.'

When she looked puzzled, he smiled and said, 'Well there ain't, is there? Figure it out. You just say you got lost on the range, met up with me and I was good enough to escort you home. Now, me being so accommodatin', you might say, don't you think that deserves at least a little kiss?'

Charlie felt another waft of his stale breath and drew away from him. Suddenly his mood changed and he seized her roughly.

'Come here, you hot little bitch!' he exclaimed.

Charlie screamed, but although she fought, kicked and scratched he was proving far too strong for her. He bore her to the ground but just as all her strength failed her, the weight of his body was suddenly removed. Through tear-filled eyes she saw the figure of another man, and heard the sickening smash of bone on bone as he struck her attacker full on the jaw.

Schulze fell backwards, his head striking a rock as he fell with a splash into the stream.

'Brad!' Charlie cried when she recognized him.

He helped her back on to her feet. The expression on his face was cold and hard.

'You OK?' he asked abruptly.

She nodded. He walked over to the stream. The water had partially revived Schulze but his head had been badly cut; the stream-water ran red with his blood.

Brad seized him by the collar and belt and hauled him out of the stream. He dropped him on the ground and disarmed him.

'There's some handcuffs in my saddle-bag, fetch them,' he ordered Charlie.

She hastened to obey him. 'Brad, I didn't give him no encouragement,' she pleaded.

'I know you didn't.' His tone was softer now. He snapped the handcuffs shut over his prisoner's wrists as he spoke.

'I had no idea you were following us,' she said, wonderingly.

'Would have been surprised iffen you did,' he said.

He bent down over Schulze, who was showing signs of recovering consciousness.

'That man is evil,' Charlie said with a shudder. 'Ever since we left Tait, I was wary of him. What do we do now?'

'I gotta get him back into town.'

'What about Tait? Hasn't he put everyone against you?'

'You bet he has,' Schulze said sullenly through his swollen lips. 'Show your face in Paradise and you're dead meat, Rio.'

★   ★   ★

Jake Griffin left the Warrenders in a state of considerable agitation. He headed straight towards the sheriff's office.

'Howdy. Jake, how's things?' Lee Rance enquired affably as Griffin entered his office. Simultaneously he leaned down and pulled open the bottom drawer of his desk to reveal the Derringer he kept there in case of emergency.

'There's things goin' on in this town I just don't understand,' Griffin said.

'How come?'

Rance listened without interruption as Griffin explained what was on his mind.

'Your case against Captain Tait is mighty thin,' he remarked when Griffin had finished. 'It relies solely on the evidence of Lisa Warrender. And I just can't imagine a grand jury committing a man for trial on the hearsay of a blind girl.'

'She recognized my voice well enough,' Griffin snapped. 'She knew who I was without being told.'

'I don't doubt she will recognize the voices of people she knows well,' Rance replied. 'But those of complete strangers? I doubt it.'

'Isn't there some way we could check Tait out? How about you sending a telegram to the Ranger HQ in Austin?'

'Aren't you forgetting something? Captain Tait has already been vouched for by Judge Banyon. It was he who sent for him after all.'

Griffin stared at the sheriff. 'I guess I was forgettin'. It was Banyon and his cronies who got you this job, wasn't it?'

'Now wait a minute . . . '

'I can see I'm gonna get nowhere with you,' Griffin said harshly. He turned for the door.

'I'm warning you, Griffin. Don't you and your friends go making any more trouble.'

Griffin paused beside the door.

'Trouble for who? I've never seen you do anything but shine the seat of your pants on that chair. You're one of these clever guys who's got more wind than a bull in green corn time. You've done nothing to find out who murdered the Warrenders. Well, I've had enough and I'm tellin' you loud and clear, I'm

176

heading back home an' when I get there I'm gonna round up the boys and we're gonna come back to Paradise for a showdown.'

'Making threats like that is against the law,' Rance said. His hand crept stealthily towards the Derringer as he spoke.

'What are you gonna do?' Griffin sneered. 'Arrest me?'

The sight of the nester turning his back in disdain forced Rance's hand. But even as he dived for the Derringer, Griffin whirled round, Colt in hand.

'Don't figure I don't know how to use this. One false move an' I'll blow you right outa that fancy chair.'

Rance froze, half-way there. His handsome face paled as Griffin advanced on him. Bile rose, stuck in his throat with a bitter taste, as the nester thrust the barrel of his Colt into his neck, forcing him back in his chair until his head hit the wall.

Griffin leaned over and picked up the Derringer.

'Shoot a man in the back, would you? Then claim he was resisting arrest? Well, I believe it's no more than I expected, I guess.'

He cocked his Colt. The click sounded unnaturally loud in the stillness of the office.

'Don't shoot!' Rance said hoarsely.

Griffin uncocked the weapon and holstered it.

'You're lucky I ain't tarred with the same brush as the likes of you,' he remarked. 'But at least now we know where we stand. If I was you, Rance, I'd get outa town pronto before I catch up with you again.'

When Griffin had left, Rance remained seated, his face sheened in perspiration. When he finally regained control of himself, he rose, strapped on his gunbelt and went outside, heading for the livery.

If Griffin is watching, he thought grimly, he'll think I'm doing as he ordered. But I guess it's high time Judge Banyon was informed about what's going on.

* ★ ★

'I guess you'd best head for home,' Brad said to Charlie as he made ready to leave with his prisoner.

She shook her head.

'Ma's got problems enough. What if Tait's men find me there? Let me come with you, please, Brad.'

'OK, but on one condition — as soon as we get there you go and stay with the Warrenders.'

'OK, Brad.'

As Brad nodded, Schulze said:

'What's with all this 'Brad', Rio? I thought your first name was Frank.'

'For your information, I'm called neither,' Brad snapped. 'My real name is Brad Saunders. Captain Brad Saunders, Texas Rangers.'

Schulze stared at him for a moment before his bloodstained features broke into a smile.

'So Tait was right all along. Hey, do you really think any one in Paradise is gonna believe you?'

179

'We'll see about that,' Brad snapped.

'So where are you gonna put me when we get into town?' Schulze asked as they approached the outskirts.

'Why, in jail, of course,' came the reply.

'Rance won't wear that.'

'If Rance don't watch out, he'll be sharin' a cell with you,' Brad snapped.

'Be like hitchin' a horse with a coyote,' Charlie said.

*　*　*

With the assistance of Little Eagle, it didn't take long before Tait discovered what Brad had done.

'There was fist-fight here,' the Indian explained, pointing to a bloodstain on the rocks. 'Then all three go this way.' He pointed towards Paradise as he spoke.

'That can only mean one thing,' Tait said. 'Rio has followed my men and the girl. You sure there's only three sets of prints?'

The Indian nodded.

'Other man, he leave early. He head for Judge Banyon's ranch. He one of the hands, I recognize his horse from sign.'

'If they've all gone to Paradise, it can mean only one thing,' Tait said. 'Rio must have tracked Schulze and got the drop on him.'

'Just who is this guy?' one of Banyon's men demanded. 'How come he can track like Little Eagle?'

There was a murmur of assent from his companions.

'We can only answer that question when we catch him,' Tait snapped. 'You ride back to your ranch and tell Banyon to bring every man he can spare with him into Paradise. The rest of you stay with me.'

'So what's Rio's game?' Dooley asked uneasily.

'I guess we'd best find out. Let's ride,' Tait said, urging his horse forward.

10

'What the hell's gotten into Jake? He must have got some news,' Sam Parks remarked as Jake Griffin galloped into Owl Creek.

'Listen boys, I guess we got it all wrong. It's Frank Rio who's the Ranger. Tait and his men are impostors.'

The small group pressed closer in to listen to Jake's account of recent events.

'I don't believe a word of it,' one of his hearers declared when he had finished.

'But you've got the girl's word. She swears it was Tait and his men who murdered her family. Rio's never harmed a hair of her head. Would a guilty man have taken care of her the way he did?'

Jake stared round desperately at the circle of disbelieving faces.

'You only got the word of the Warrender girl,' Sam Parks said. 'No disrespect, Jake, but if she didn't see anything, how could any jury convict Tait and his men?'

'Are you sayin' she's a liar?' Jake said hotly.

'Easy, now, Jake. I ain't saying that. What I am sayin' is that the evidence against Tait being what he says he is is mighty slim. After all, Lisa Warrender's only a kid. And what if we're wrong and Tait truly is a Ranger? Where does that leave us?'

There was a low murmur of assent from the group.

'Won't you ride into town and check it out with me?' Jake pleaded.

'Sorry, Jake, but we got things to do. Word is Cowper's men are out fencing. You're on your own on this one,' came the reply.

'OK, if that's the way you want it. I'm gonna ride straight back into Paradise. My horse is nearly all in, I could use a remount.

'OK, have it your own way,' he said, when there was no reply.

★ ★ ★

Brad and Charlie parted company on the outskirts of Paradise.

'Now mind you go straight to the Warrenders,' he told her.

She nodded.

'You take care of yourself, Brad,' she urged.

He responded with a nod. He pinned his Texas Rangers badge on to the lapel of his jacket so it could easily be seen.

His slow ride along the town's main street with his handcuffed prisoner in tow achieved just what he intended. The news ran ahead like a rampant prairie-fire, bringing people in scores out on to the boardwalks to watch his passage.

He dismounted outside the sheriff's office, tethered both mounts to the hitching rail and, gun in hand prodded his prisoner on to the boardwalk. The single shot he fired to shatter the lock on the door brought even more people out on to the street.

Brad lost no time in locking Schulze into one of the cells. He had completed that task and returned to the office when the door opened, somewhat tentatively, to reveal a corpulent, well-dressed man.

'Step inside and state your business,' Brad snapped.

'I'm Nathan Cowper, mayor of this town. I see you've just locked up one of Captain Tait's men. Just what do you think you're about?'

He listened in silence as Brad gave him an account of the situation. 'If you want to verify my credentials, all you have to do is telegraph Austin,' Brad said in conclusion.

'Now wait a minute, do you seriously expect me to believe that Judge Banyon has brought in an impostor?' Cowper said with a splutter.

In his own mind, Cowper was jubilant. If this quiet-spoken man was who he said he was, then this was his big chance to bring down Banyon for good.

'Like I said,' Brad reiterated. 'Go send a wire to Austin. Enquire about both of us, if you like, but I know what the answer will be.'

The door opened and another man appeared.

'Who are you?' Brad snapped.

'I'm David Fife, manager of the Lazy Z. What's going on, Nathan?'

Before Brad could reply, the door was thrust open again. 'Cap'n Tait's comin',' was the terse piece of information rendered.

Brad thrust his way between the pencil-slim David Fife and Nathan Cowper's bulk. There was a gasp from the assembled crowd as he appeared on the boardwalk. Two hundred yards away, a group of horsemen were approaching at a fast trot with Tait at their head. As they came closer in, Tait drew clear; the rest, with Dooley at their head, reined in.

The faces of the crowd looked puzzled as the two men, both wearing the same badge, confronted each other.

'How come you're wearin' that badge, Rio?' Tait leaned forward in his saddle as he spoke.

'Because I'm the only one of us who is entitled to do so,' Brad replied evenly.

The attentive crowd exploded into a frenzy of speculative discussion.

'You're an impostor,' Tait declared. He pointed his finger at Brad. 'Everyone in this town knows that's so.'

'Only on your say-so.' Brad made no effort to disguise the contempt in his voice as he spoke.

'You're a liar. I'm gonna arrest you for murder.' Tait's voice rose, inadvertently betraying his insecurity in the face of Brad's calmness.

'Wait a minute,' a voice shouted out from the crowd. 'Just what did this guy say to you, Mr Mayor?'

The boardwalk creaked as Nathan Cowper moved forward. He was sweating heavily and was obviously ill at ease.

'So which of 'em *do* we believe?' Cowper was asked when he had come to a halt.

'If you are in doubt, then let me tell you.'

The crowd fell silent in the hot, dusty street as a clear voice rang out.

'Lisa!' Brad muttered under his breath.

For the next few moments there was no sound save that of the tap-tap of a stick as, with Charlie Lister following a few paces behind, Lisa made her way across the street towards the sheriff's office.

The crowd watched her, parting to allow her through. She shrugged aside the sympathetic hands that tried to guide her on to the steps up to the boardwalk. Unnerringly, she made her way to Brad's side. There she stopped and turned her sightless eyes towards the people.

'It's said that the only evidence against Tait and his men is that of a blind person and that it cannot be relied on. We have five senses: sight, touch, taste, smell and . . . hearing. An Indian can find his quarry using eyesight that he has developed to a far higher degree than a normal man. Because I am blind, my sense of hearing is developed to a far greater extent than yours. And I know that the man who murdered my family is the man who calls himself Captain Tait.'

The utter conviction in the girl's calm voice riveted the crowd. For a few moments utter silence reigned.

'Why, Tait, you evil, double-crossing coyote!'

The shout triggered a deep-throated, angry roar from the crowd. Even as it surged towards Tait, his gun appeared in his hand.

Brad's attention was so occupied with the girl he was a fraction late in drawing his own weapon. Too late, he realized that the outlaw's target was Lisa. The bullet struck her and as she collapsed like a rag doll alongside him,

Brad's whole world seemed to disintegrate.

In the commotion that followed, Tait made good his escape. Dooley was not so fortunate. He was dragged off his horse by the angry crowd and disappeared underneath a welter of flailing fists and boots.

Sensing a lynching in the air, Brad bellowed 'Hold it!' He took out his gun and loosed a shot into the air. It took several minutes to restore order, during which time he ensured the battered and bleeding Dooley had joined Schulze in the cells.

When Brad returned to the sidewalk his worst fear was realized. Charlie was standing over Lisa's inert body. Brad didn't have to ask, for the distraught look on Charlie's face told him that Lisa was dying.

The onlookers parted and stood back as he bent down over her.

'Lisa,' he said hoarsely.

'Captain Saunders,' she said in a voice so quiet that he had to put his ear over her mouth to catch the words.

'I spoke the truth and they believed me . . . '

As her head fell back, Brad stood up and looked about him. Anger welled up inside him, the ferocity of which he had not felt for a long time.

'Where's Tait?' he demanded harshly.

'I guess he got clean away,' Cowper reported.

Brad leapt to his feet with an explosion of oaths.

'Did anyone see which way Tait went?' he demanded.

'He went back the way he came.' Charlie caught hold of Brad's arm as she spoke. 'Take care, Brad, won't you?'

As he looked down into her tear-stained face for one brief moment he felt his resolve weaken, but then he caught sight of two men carrying Lisa's lifeless body on a makeshift stretcher and he became sharply focused again.

He left the boardwalk and shouldered his way through the crowd to the hitching rail. He untethered Blaze and swung into the saddle. The crowd watched quietly as he set forth at a canter along the street.

'Hey, mister, you lookin' fer that guy who just left in an all-fired hurry? Well, just keep right on goin'.'

Brad responded to the information volunteered by an old-timer by urging Blaze forward. Once clear of the town, the horizon was unobstructed, and, looking along the trail he could see the dust-cloud raised by his quarry.

But what caught his eye also was the even bigger dust-cloud approaching Tait along the same trail.

Banyon! It could only be Banyon!

What would happen when Tait met up with him?

Brad reined in. He took out his spyglass and focused it, watching the events taking place ahead as if he were in the audience at a play. Tait and Banyon met, conversed with each other, and then the entire group advanced towards him.

Brad waited, sitting motionless in the

saddle until Banyon had caught sight of him. He remained so until Banyon and his men drew level.

'I believe I have a prisoner for you,' Banyon said with a dust-caked smile.

Brad smiled grimly. Banyon was every bit as smart as he expected him to be.

'I understand he took a shot at you and killed the Warrender girl by mistake,' Banyon continued. 'May I suggest that we escort him into town together and incarcerate him in jail where he belongs? And then I believe we must lose no time in bringing him and his men to a trial over which I shall be more than happy to preside.'

Brad glanced at Tait. The temptation to wipe the smile of triumph off the man's face was overwhelming. The plan was transparent. With Lisa dead, in his capacity as judge, Banyon would contrive to secure his release.

Brad kept his own counsel as the group returned to Paradise. The crowd, satiated with enough incident for one day, had dispersed by the time he re-entered the town. They rode straight to the sheriff's office where David Fife was still keeping watch. Jake Griffin, who had recently arrived from Owl Creek, was with him.

'So you've caught him?' Fife exclaimed as Brad ushered Tait into the office.

'I believe that I and my men were to prove of some assistance to Captain Saunders,' Judge Banyon said with a smile.

Tait, who had obviously been briefed to say nothing, went meekly into the cells and Brad turned the key.

'There's just one piece of unfinished business,' Brad remarked.

'And what is that?' Judge Banyon asked pleasantly. 'Haven't you achieved enough for one day?'

Brad ignored him. 'Mr Fife, did you believe that Tait was a Texas Ranger?'

Fife look surprised. Then he said, 'Why, yes, of course, we all did.'

'And who exactly told you who Tait was?'

'Why, Judge Banyon, of course. He

told Nathan Cowper and myself one day at the Cattlemen's Club that he had asked the Texas Rangers to settle our dispute with the nesters over our wiring off the range.'

At this point they were joined by Nathan Cowper. He was clutching a telegraph flimsy.

'Well?' Banyon demanded.

'I've just had confirmation from Austin saying that Captain Saunders is a Texas Ranger. It appears that he has been sent here at the request of the State Governor to investigate certain complaints raised by Bill Warrender.'

Brad turned to Banyon. 'So what does that say to you about Tait?'

Banyon shrugged. 'I acted in good faith. When he and his men arrived wearing Texas Ranger badges I saw no reason to question the authorities in Austin about it. I assumed he had been sent to deal with the situation.'

'With a situation of your making?' Griffin demanded. 'How do you make that out?'

'Banyon, your big talk doesn't impress me,' Brad said. 'I figure you knew exactly what you were doing. You brought in Tait to create a reign of terror under false pretences. Anyone who stood up to you was gonna be wiped out and no questions would be asked because you were part of the legal system. It's people like you the Governor has asked me to grub out, root and branch.'

The tension in the sheriff's office was tangible. Banyon stared at Brad, his face contorted with fury.

Suddenly, he snapped. His hand dived inside his jacket but even as it was withdrawn, holding a Derringer, Brad's gun was already out. The boom of the Colt in the confined space sounded shockingly loud. Banyon's Derringer discharged harmlessly into the floor as he fell, shot through the heart. For a few moments, there was stunned silence. Brad broke it, when he said:

'Gentlemen, now that I have shot Judge Banyon in self-defence, I believe my business here is finished.'

He strode out of the office and mounted Blaze. As he rode round to the Warrenders' house, people lounging on the sidewalks eyed him with a combination of awe and respect.

Charlie opened the door to his knock. Her eyes, red with weeping, came alive when she saw it was him. But out of respect for the grieving couple within, she kept her welcome muted.

'I told Lisa not to go,' Hester Warrender said bleakly when she saw Brad.

'She did what she needed to do,' Brad replied. 'We have to respect that. The Governor is determined to see law and order established in Texas. Tait and his men will rot in jail before they hang for what they did. You have my word on that.'

'But what about Lisa's testimony, now that she is dead?' Jacob Warrender raised his tear-stained face to Brad as he spoke.

'She gave her testimony in the presence of the people,' Brad replied. 'What greater witness can she give?'

★ ★ ★

Brad stayed on in Paradise for Lisa's funeral. He organized meetings with both sides involved in the bitter dispute. All the parties agreed that with tact and commonsense they could live side by side without acrimony.

Sheriff Rance had disappeared and was formally removed from office. Brad's help and advice was sought in the selection procedure to appoint a successor.

Jess Collier had survived his wound and indicated his willingness to incriminate his erstwhile employer.

'I will give evidence against Tait in any court in the land,' David Fife told Brad.

He was not short of supporters, for public fury at Lisa's murder drove many other citizens to intimate their willingness to bear witness to her denunciation of Tait.

And there was Charlie.

'I guess you'll be leaving town after the funeral?' she said.

Brad nodded. 'I'll have to escort the prisoners to the state penitentiary and make my report.'

'But you will write to me?'

He nodded. 'Sure, I will.'

'Maybe one day you'll stop by in Paradise again?'

He smiled and kissed her. 'Just let anyone try and stop me.'

'I love you, Brad,' she said. 'I'll wait as long as it takes.'

The whole town turned out for Lisa's funeral. Everyone, united at last, listened in silence as the clergyman expressed the hope that she and her family had not died in vain and that law and order would now be restored after the tragedy in this town so peculiarly named 'Paradise'.